BATTLE OF KILLERS!

Long Rider heard a snarl. Looking up, he saw the cougar he had been tracking. The cat was crouched down low, its belly pressed against the ridge. It snarled again, its lips drawing back over its sharp teeth, its whiskers flickering and its yellow eyes narrowing.

Long Rider slowly raised his rifle and took aim at the cat crouched directly above him. Before he could fire, the cougar launched itself into the air, the sharp claws of its front paws outstretched.

Long Rider fired, a wild shot which missed its target. Before he could fire a second time, he lost his rifle as the cougar landed on him. . . .

DON'T MISS THESE
AUTHENTIC WESTERN SERIES
FROM THE BERKLEY PUBLISHING GROUP

FURY by Jim Austin
Meet John Fury. Gunfighter. Legend. Where there's trouble, there's Fury.

THE HORSEMEN by Gary McCarthy
The epic story of a frontier family's glorious dream, raising horses in the untamed West.

NORTHWEST DESTINY by Bill Gulick
The award-winning author's acclaimed trilogy of white men and Indians bound by blood.

SONS OF TEXAS by Tom Early
"A series that brings to mind L'Amour's Sackett family saga."—*Booklist*

SHILOH by Dalton Walker
The classic adventures of a Civil War veteran turned bounty hunter.

LONG RIDER by Clay Dawson
A white man raised by Indians. Long Rider was caught between the blood and hate of two peoples.

CREED by Bryce Harte
Based on actual records, this epic series captures life in a Texas town shattered by the Civil War.

BROTHERS IN BLOOD by Daniel St. James
On the Canadian border, a U.S. Marshal and a Canadian Mountie are bound by a loyalty only brothers can share.

Westerns by Giles Tippette
The new star of the classic western novel, Tippette captures the American dream in the saga of the Williams clan.

LONG RIDER

★ GUNS AND GOLD ★

CLAY DAWSON

DIAMOND BOOKS, NEW YORK

This book is a Diamond original edition,
and has never been previously published.

GUNS AND GOLD

A Diamond Book / published by arrangement with
the author

PRINTING HISTORY
Diamond edition / August 1993

ISBN: 1-55773-926-9

Diamond Books are published by The Berkley Publishing Group,
200 Madison Avenue, New York, New York 10016.
The name "DIAMOND" and its logo
are trademarks belonging to Charter Communications, Inc.

PRINTED IN THE UNITED STATES OF AMERICA

10 9 8 7 6 5 4 3 2 1

LONG RIDER
★ GUNS AND GOLD ★

CHAPTER ONE

Gabe Conrad squinted against the glare of the sun from the snowcapped peaks of the Sierra Nevada Mountains as he rode through a sheltered valley beneath them. The peaks glistened with their mantles of ice and snow like jagged jewels, frosty diamonds gleaming in the spring sun.

Gabe looked away from the mountains and the cloudless blue sky they seemed to be trying to pierce and gazed out across the meadow that spread out in front of him. The meadow was covered with a tangled profusion of colorful wildflowers, stirring in the light breeze that was blowing across the rough land.

He sat easy in the saddle, his strong hands relaxed on the reins that were looped around them, and let his gray gelding pick its way through the flowers and around the scattered crumbled remains of cracked boulders.

He rode a trail that paralleled the Nevada state line miles away on his left as he headed east through the mountains. On one side of the valley rugged cliffs of limestone rose and on the other a thick stand of pines climbed a steep slope that rose almost perpendicular to the earth beneath it. A meadowlark sang somewhere within the shelter of the pines, a shy performer in the early morning stillness.

Gabe Conrad was a wiry, muscular man who had clearly spent a lifetime under the open sky. The exposed skin of his face and hands showed signs of weathering. There were wrinkles at the corners of his eyes and less visible ones around the corners of his mouth. He was a man in his prime, one whose gray eyes were accustomed to studying whatever trail he happened to be traveling and the countryside surrounding it, alert to any kind of threat—an enraged grizzly, a trigger-happy gunman. The grayness of his eyes made them seem pale. But for all their apparent paleness, they were piercing, and many a man had found himself forced to look away when they focused on him. In fear. Or awe.

His chest and shoulders were broad, his limbs were lean, and his waist was narrow. His lips formed a thin line above his strong square chin. His long hair was the color of sand at the bottom of a creek bed.

His clothes were dusty from the trail and well-worn. They consisted of a linen duster, a blue denim shirt, jeans tucked into down-at-the-heels and badly scuffed black boots, and an almost shapeless black felt slouch hat.

To shield his eyes from the glare of the rising sun, he pulled his hat down low on his forehead. His gray nickered softly as it stumbled over a fragment of stone and then plodded on.

On Gabe's right hip, its butt forward for a fast cross draw, hung a Frontier Model Colt .44 in its holster. In his saddle scabbard rested a '73 Winchester. The gun belt he wore strapped around his waist contained .44-40 cartridges in its leather loops. The same ammunition fed both his rifle and his side arm.

A sudden movement off to his right caught his eye. He turned his head and saw the meadowlark he had heard earlier leave the cover of the stand of pines and fly out over the meadow directly ahead of him. The bird's brown body, streaked with black, glided on the breeze, its yellow breast which bore a black crescent clearly visible. The meadowlark dropped down to the ground and disappeared from sight.

Gabe rode on, the spot where the lark had vanished directly in his path. He kept his eyes on it, almost certain of what he would find when he reached it. He guided his gray to the left and then, when he was within range of the spot he had kept his eyes on, he saw it: a domed nest built on the ground. Perched atop it was the male meadowlark and now, at Gabe's approach, the bird began to chatter and then to screech, flapping its wings, trying to frighten off the intruder who threatened the safety of the nest.

When the female emerged from the nest to add its shrieking to that of its mate, Gabe managed to catch a glimpse of the four white eggs, speckled with red, which rested in the nest and which would, in nature's own good time, hatch four more meadowlarks.

He skirted the nest which he recognized as not only a sign of spring but also a herald of the summer that was on its way. Only when he had traveled on for a distance of more than forty yards did the screeching of the male and female meadowlarks diminish and finally fade away into silence.

That silence was broken by the rumbling of Gabe's gut as hunger grew within him. He tried at first to ignore it, but soon found that it would not be ignored. He tried taking a drink from his battered canteen that hung by a leather thong from his saddle horn. It worked—for a few minutes—and then the rumbling returned, louder now.

"I could eat a horse," he said aloud. "But I won't," he quickly added, stroking his gray's sweaty neck.

He covered another several miles through the mountains, enduring the nagging hunger, before he spotted a stand of great burdock off to his right. The plants were easily recognizable—long stalks, growing in groups of three. He turned his horse and headed for them. The sight of them—their flower heads resembling oblong hearts which were rough and purplish with clearly defined leaves—made his mouth water, although he would have much preferred a meal of meat. But he had seen no sign of game along the trail during the entire morning.

When he reached the great burdock plants, he drew rein and dismounted. He pulled out his knife and, after choosing some year-old plants, distinguishable by their lack of flowers or burrs, he pulled them up out of the ground and cut off their roots which he rubbed in his hands to rid them of as much dirt as possible. Then he peeled them as if they were parsnips. Next, he stripped the leaves from the plants' long stalks and placed them on the ground next to the roots. He used his knife to strip the stalks of their bitter skins and then hunkered down to make a meal of his harvest.

His gray swung its head and nuzzled his neck. He held up one of the roots, and the gelding took it from him and began to chew. Its lips and teeth worked vigorously as it devoured the root.

Gabe chewed on a root, and when it was gone he ate some of the leaves. He saved the stalks for last. Later, while savoring them in small pieces, he remembered how his mother had learned to make a kind of candy from the stalks of great burdock plants.

He could taste that candy now in his memory, the candy his mother had made from the pith of the stalks, the candy she had learned to make under the tutelage of the women of the Oglala Sioux. Other memories of his boyhood came rushing back to him as he continued to eat, his eyes open but not seeing the reality of the world around him. He saw instead that other world, the one he and his mother had lived in after having been taken prisoner by the Oglala, the People. Some of the scenes which came flooding through his mind were pleasant. But some were painful. Like the one his mother had told

him about in blunt detail. The one that happened only
an hour after he was conceived, the last time his parents
would ever make love. It was the scene of the battle in
which his parents had tried to fight off the Oglala band
that had attacked their wagon train. His father had died in
that battle, a stone-tipped lance embedded in his bloody
chest. His mother had been taken captive, and Gabe was
born and raised among the Oglala.

Gabe closed his eyes. In the darkness he saw other
sights. Hunting parties. Winter in the Oglala villages.
Boyhood games like ice-sledding in which he of all
the boys participating had often slid the farthest. The
sticking-together game in which both boys and girls
joined in to see which of the tops that they set to spinning on the ice would outbump and outspin all the
others.

He remembered the Night Dances around the campfires
to celebrate a marriage or success in the hunt. He could
see the young women attired in their finest deerskin
dresses, the young men adorned in bright paints and
wearing elegant deerskin sashes.

Gabe smiled to himself, lost in mostly pleasant memories. He had lived among the Oglala until he was four-
teen when his mother had insisted that he leave the
People and go out into the white world and learn to
live in it. He had hated her for sending him away but
later learned the wisdom of what she had done. But had
he learned to live in the white world? To a degree, yes.
But he still felt himself, in his heart of hearts, to be a
part of the People and their ways.

The breeze grew stronger, reminding Gabe of Tate,
the Wind, who was one of the People's gods. Tate, he
recalled, was said by the People to live at the entrance to
the Spirit World and it was there, that his wife, Ite, bore
him quadruplets: the North, the South, the East, and the
West Winds. Tate had traveled with him the time he had
made the grueling ride through a blizzard that had given

him the name Long Rider. He had ridden two horses to death during that long journey on which he was accompanied only by Tate who sometimes whispered and sometimes screamed in his ears as he rode at a fast and furious pace to warn a distant Oglala village of a planned attack upon it by the United States cavalry.

He saved the lives of the people of that village and was honored with the name Long Rider to commemorate the feat he had so successfully performed.

He whispered a greeting now to Tate as he remained hunkered down in the shadow of his gray and offered words of prayer to *Wakan-tanka,* the Great Spirit who ruled the world. He did not ask *Wakan-tanka* to keep him safe. He did not ask to be given riches or even peace. He asked instead that he be allowed to live the kind of life that would make him worthy of *Wakan-tanka's* care and concern.

He rose and tossed aside the last of his makeshift meal of great burdock. His hunger, although not entirely satisfied, had at least been tamed for the time being. His stomach no longer rumbled. But visions of roast venison taunted him as he swung into the saddle and moved his gray out.

They were crossing a stretch of land dotted with rocky hummocks sometime later when Gabe caught a glimpse of something moving up ahead, something that moved too swiftly between the slopes of two adjoining hummocks for him to be able to identify it.

But it had been some sort of animal. Meat.

It had been too large to have been a rabbit, too bulky to have been a bird. Cougar, he decided, and discovered moments later that he had been right in his speculation when the catamount came into view ahead of him. The cat moved slowly but with a controlled intensity. Its sleek hide rippled as its muscles moved beneath it. It did not turn its head to look in Gabe's direction which might mean that it hadn't seen—or smelled—him. Tate, the Wind, was journeying from east to west and, Gabe guessed, carrying his scent away from the beast with the tawny hide. From where he sat his saddle, having reined in his gray at the first sight of the cougar, he could see its whiskers twitching and its nostrils quivering.

The animal was hunting.

The gray moved beneath Gabe. It circled to the right, then back again. It stamped its front hooves. It lowered its head, its nostrils twitching.

"You smell him, do you?" Gabe asked softly. "He makes you nervous, does he?"

The gray tossed its head.

"Don't fret. We're more than a match for that critter," he whispered to the gelding as he withdrew his rifle from its saddle scabbard.

The cougar was now nowhere in sight.

Gabe put heels to his horse, and the animal stepped forward but not without offering some slight resistance. He stroked its neck, whispered to it to quiet it down, but he knew that he was not likely to be successful, not with the scent of catamount riding in on the wind.

When he reached the spot where he had last seen the cougar, he drew rein and, as his gray balked, kept a tight grip on the reins and scanned the ground.

Tracks. To the right. Leading south. He turned his horse and began to follow the cat's trail which ran roughly parallel to a wide river on his right only to lose it five minutes later when he reached a sloping limestone formation where the tracks were no longer visible. He dismounted and, carrying his rifle, climbed the slope. From its summit, he surveyed the land below him. The river wound its way toward the slope and flowed turbulently directly below it, running into a steep waterfall approximately half a mile away. He saw no trace of the cougar. Down below on the far side of the small mountain were flatlands covered with grasses.

Squinting from the glare of the sun that was now almost directly overhead, Gabe scanned the area, searching for sign of the mountain lion. He saw none. It was as if the cat had melted completely away, leaving no trace of itself behind. He was about to turn and climb back down the slope when he saw movement almost directly below him. It had been so slight, so nearly unnoticeable, that, for a moment, he thought his eyes might have deceived him.

But no, there it was again—a stirring of the grass that had not been caused by the wind. He kept his eyes on the spot. Minutes passed. He raised his rifle to his shoulder, sighting down on the spot, his finger on the trigger, ready to pull it the instant the cougar showed itself.

It was not the cougar which ultimately showed itself but a bighorn sheep. The animal rose up out of the grass like an apparition. For a moment, its liquid eyes seemed to come to rest on Gabe. His finger tightened on the trigger. He was about to squeeze off a shot—sheep tasted just as good, if not better, than the meat of catamount when properly roasted—but the bighorn loped away. Almost leisurely. It seemed to be in no great hurry. In fact, it halted not far from the place where it had made its initial appearance and looked back.

Gabe shifted his rifle barrel so that he was once again sighting on his prey. Again his finger tightened on the trigger. But the bighorn loped away—back toward the ridge on which Gabe was standing. It halted when it was about thirty yards away from Gabe, then began to climb the ridge.

Gabe fired.

His shot struck the limestone ridge directly behind the bighorn which had begun to climb more quickly as if it sensed the danger it was in. Gabe swung the barrel of his rifle again, tracking his quarry, and fired a second time.

This time his round hit the target. The bighorn's head snapped to one side as Gabe's bullet slammed into its heart. The animal's bulky body shuddered and then, incredibly, it took another series of short steps as it continued its ascent and blood began to flow from the small entrance wound in its side.

Gabe, his rifle butt still pressed against his shoulder, tracked the sheep, ready to fire again if necessary.

The bighorn's front legs suddenly buckled beneath it. It went down on its knees with its hindquarters still up in the air. Then it fell and rolled over to lay twitching, all four of its legs jerking back and forth.

By the time Gabe reached the spot where the animal lay on the side of the slope, it was dead. He stood there for a moment, looking down at the dead sheep, his mouth watering. Then, cradling his rifle in one arm, he reached down with his free hand and got a good grip on one of the animal's curved horns. He turned and began to drag his trophy up the slope. He halted when he heard a snarl. Looking up, he saw the cougar that had vanished when he had been tracking it earlier. The cat was crouched down low, its belly pressed against the ridge. It snarled again, its lips drawing back over its sharp teeth, its whiskers flickering and its yellow eyes narrowing.

Gabe released his hold on the sheep's horn. With the carcass lying at his feet, he slowly raised his rifle and took aim at the cat crouched directly above him. But before he could fire, the cougar launched itself into the air, the sharp claws of its front paws outstretched.

Gabe fired, a wild shot which missed its target. Before he could fire a second time, he lost his rifle as the cougar landed on him and brought him down to the ground.

Together man and beast rolled down the limestone slope until they reached level ground. Then Gabe was instantly up on his hands and knees, scrambling frantically away from his snarling attacker. The cougar flung out its right front paw, and its claws ripped Gabe's duster without doing any damage to the man who wore it.

Gabe sprang to his feet and began to hastily back away from the mountain lion which was crouched down on the ground again and staring up at him. As he stepped backward—a single step—the cat inched along the ground toward him. He halted. So did the cat. He took another backward step, reaching for his Colt as he did so. The cougar crept closer to him, its wet fangs glistening in the sunlight.

His six-gun cleared leather. As it did so, the cat sprang at him with a shrill sound that could only be called a scream. Gabe fired his .44 and hit the mountain lion in the right front leg. But the momentum of its spring carried it onward, and the cat struck Gabe with the force of a battering ram, sending his hat flying and knocking his gun to the ground before he could fire again. He went down again and this time, when he tried to roll away from his attacker, he could not do so. He was, he discovered, pinned to the ground beneath the surprisingly great weight of the catamount.

He twisted his head to the side as the animal's fangs flashed downward toward his face. He felt them fasten on his shoulder through the jacket he was wearing and heard it tear when the cougar withdrew. Before it could go for him again, he swung his right arm and struck the side of its head, snapping it to one side. But the animal was not deterred by the tactic. It tried again to fasten its fangs in Gabe—this time in his throat—and it failed to do so only because, as those gleaming teeth descended, Gabe seized the beast and threw it from him.

The cougar recovered quickly, standing with saliva dripping from its open jaws, its eyes gleaming as it warily watched the man it clearly intended to kill.

Gabe grabbed a handful of limestone dust and shreds of grass he ripped from the ground. He threw the debris at the cougar. When the feline shrank back from the onslaught, blinking and coughing as some of the dirt entered its eyes and open mouth, Gabe lunged for his dropped gun. He was inches from the weapon when the cougar flew forward, all four of its feet off the ground, and landed directly in front of his reaching hand. He hastily withdrew it, but not before the cougar, with a swift swoop of one paw, raked the back of his hand, drawing blood.

Gabe cursed and leapt to his feet. As the cat prepared to leap at him again, he raised one foot and then, when the animal did spring, he booted it in the lower jaw, sending it flying backward, head over thrashing heels. The catamount hit the ground with a loud thud but was almost immediately up on all fours and stalking Gabe again. It crouched low, its yellow eyes never shifting from its chosen prey, as it moved forward.

Gabe stepped back toward a fist-sized rock that had been broken off a boulder by the alternate freezing and thawing of the stone formation in the harshness of the mountain winters. He never looked directly at the stone but kept his eyes on the cat which was still intently stalking him. But he could see the missile as he came closer to it out of the corner of his eye.

When he was within a foot of it, he quickly stooped and swooped it up in his right hand. This time when the cougar went for him, blood spraying from its wounded leg, he was ready for it. He raised the rock in his hand high above his head and then brought it down with all the force he could muster, aiming for the cougar's skull. But he missed his target. The rock struck the cougar's shoulder as it shifted position slightly, scraping it raw but doing no serious damage to the animal.

Once again, as the mountain lion landed on him, Gabe was knocked to the ground where again he battled his feline adversary with fists and feet and even teeth. He bit savagely into the cat's shoulder while simultaneously striking it with a series of blows, a tattoo of stiffly clenched fists.

The cougar, dazed from the onslaught, scrambled away from him, blinking and growling harshly deep in its throat.

"Come on," Gabe muttered, regaining his feet and retrieving the stone that had fallen to the ground. "Come on, you bastard, I dare you!"

The cat didn't move a muscle, didn't even blink.

Gabe threw the rock. It hit the cougar directly between the eyes before falling to the ground. The animal screamed again, a shrill, nerve-racking sound. But it did not attack. Instead it staggered backward, shaking its head from side to side, one of its eyes partially closed and dripping blood.

Gabe sprang forward, intending to take advantage of the beast's confusion. He retrieved the rock and raised it high above his head. The cat looked up. The rock came down. It smashed into the animal's skull.

The cat moaned. Its eyes glazed.

Gabe, standing his ground and panting as his chest heaved and sweat streamed down his face, watched the cougar sink to the ground where it lay without moving. Cautiously, he approached it. He nudged it gingerly with one foot. When it didn't move, he stepped back and drew a deep breath which he let out with a sigh. He dropped the bloody rock he had used as a weapon. He skirted the limp body of his adversary and went over to where his side arm was lying on the ground. He picked it up, holstered it, grabbed his hat, and then climbed the slope, heading for the spot where he had left the carcass of the bighorn sheep.

He bent down when he reached his kill and gripped one of its horns. Heaving it up off the ground, he began to drag it up the limestone slope toward the spot where he had earlier lost his rifle during his battle with the mountain lion. Pausing only for a moment when he reached his destination, he recovered his rifle and carried it in his free hand as he continued his ascent.

He had almost reached the summit of the ridge when he thought he heard something. He halted, his body stiffening, as he listened. He could hear the roar of the river down below on the far side of the ridge. But that was not what he had heard. Or had it been? He wasn't sure. He looked to the left and to the right. Nothing.

He heard it again—a kind of sharp scraping sound. He spun around to stare in shocked disbelief at the cougar he thought he had killed as it came stalking in a limping crawl up the slope behind him. He swore and backed up, swiftly putting distance between himself and what he was beginning to think of as an immortal cat.

It growled as it continued its pursuit of him. Its yellow eyes, one reddened by congealing blood, were fixed on its prey. The wound on its leg still dripped blood, leaving a red trail in its wake. The cougar limped, favoring its wounded leg.

Gabe tossed his hat aside and raised his rifle. His finger gripped the trigger. He held the weapon at hip level as he gritted his teeth and his finger squeezed the trigger. . . .

The cougar sprang at him.

His rifle roared. But the round went under the body of the leaping cat. Dodging the attacking cougar, he scrambled backward, his boots slipping on the steep slope as he did so. He almost went down when he momentarily lost his footing. The catamount landed less than a foot in front of him.

As it swung a paw in an attempt to claw him, he leaped back out of its reach. For a brief moment he considered abandoning the bighorn he had killed and letting the cougar have it. But something within him rebelled at the thought of giving up what was rightfully his. He tightened his grip on the horn of the sheep and stepped backward. Again he brought his gun up, prepared to finish the cougar once and for all. A single well-placed shot in the chest should do it. . . .

The cougar suddenly scuttled forward, dislodging loose gravel which clattered down the side of the slope. Its progress was nevertheless steady and swift.

Gabe fired but managed only to wound the animal again, this time in the shoulder. A far from fatal shot. He resisted the urge to turn and run in the face of the cat's relentless pursuit.

But when the cougar increased its pace and Gabe saw its body tense and its jaw open wide, he knew it was about to attack again. He was about to fire, but this time he did lose his balance as some of the limestone beneath his boots gave way, crumbling into gravel. He went down, his buttocks hitting the ground hard. He managed to hold onto his rifle, but before he could steady himself and fire at the cat that was racing toward him now, the cougar sprang at him. He managed to roll out of its way, and the mountain lion fell short of its goal. As Gabe scrambled to his feet and ran to the summit of the slope, the cat went after him, its feet scrabbling along the treacherous limestone.

This time when it sprang, Gabe did fire. His shot ripped into the belly of the beast. He saw the red cavity his round had made in the creature's body.

But that body, as if driven by some supernatural force, continued to fly through the air toward him. He scrambled backward.

His efforts were unsuccessful. The cat landed on him, driving him backward and onto a limestone ledge that jutted out over the river rushing by beneath him. He staggered under the awesome weight of the animal, almost fell, and struggled desperately to maintain his balance while the cat's claws tried to tear open his throat. He fought to bring the barrel of his rifle up.

But, before he could do so, he heard a loud cracking sound. He felt the ledge beneath his feet lurch, buckle, and begin to give way. He tried to tear himself free of the catamount, using his rifle as a club to do so. But the animal, with one swift swipe of a paw, knocked the rifle out of his hand. It went flying down to the ground where it skidded along the ledge until it was out of reach.

With a resounding snapping sound, the ledge gave way and sent man and cat tumbling through the air that was now filled with limestone debris. They plummeted downward, striking the surface of the river together, both of them going under the water at the same time.

Gabe managed to fight his way back to the surface. As his head broke into the open air, he gasped for breath while the strong current, largely the result of the spring melt in the mountains, twisted and twirled him along with it as it roiled toward the waterfall in the distance.

He caught a glimpse of the cougar. It was tumbling through the water, a helpless victim of the river's power. Soon it was far away from him, heading toward the roaring waterfall.

Gabe swam, not with grace but with arms desperately flailing and legs kicking. He soon found that he could hardly move his legs as his boots became waterlogged. He tried to compensate for that fact by striving even harder with his arms as he fought his way through the current toward the riverbank at the base of the limestone ledge. But for every foot he covered, the raging river forced him back as much as two feet. His lungs were burning and the blood was drumming in his head as he continued struggling to survive.

He heard a scream and glanced to his right. The cougar must have sensed its impending fate. Its head was barely above water as it was swept closer and closer to the edge of the waterfall. It tried to scream again, but its head went under the water's surface and no sound came from its mouth. It reappeared briefly, its front paws clawing the air, and then it went over the waterfall and disappeared from sight.

Gabe fought on. But the current was strong, much stronger than a man whose waterlogged boots were dragging him down and whose heart seemed about to burst as a result of his intense efforts to reach the bank. His flailing arms propelled him through the water, but the bank seemed to recede from him instead of coming closer.

When he spotted the exposed roots of a cedar at the edge of the riverbank, he fought his way toward them. They would, if he could get a good enough grip on them, keep him from being dragged downstream and over the waterfall. Gasping, occasionally gagging as river water flooded his mouth from time to time, he swam on, using every ounce of energy he could muster to fight the river's raging current.

He had never wanted anything so much in his life as he wanted to get his hands on the exposed roots of that cedar. Those roots filled his vision and were his entire world as he continued struggling. He had almost reached his goal—was reaching desperately for the roots with both hands—when a dislodged sapling came twisting toward him on the roily surface of the current.

It struck him with sufficient force to tear him away from the cedar's roots and send him bobbing helplessly downstream toward the waterfall.

CHAPTER TWO

The branches of the sapling seemed to be trying to seize Gabe. As he fought to keep his head above water, he pushed and kicked at the young tree to work his way free of it as its momentum carried him toward the waterfall.

The branches tore at his face. He was finally forced to dive down into the muddy depths of the river to escape the sapling. He held his breath, his cheeks puffing out as he did so, and treaded water until the tree, a multibranched shadow above him, disappeared from sight. Then, with a strong push downward with both arms, he propelled himself to the surface where he dog-paddled as he tried to regain his bearings. He blinked water out of his eyes, but mud had entered and irritated them so that he could hardly see his hand in front of his face. Squinting, he located the riverbank but saw no sign of the cedar tree he had been trying to reach. A minute or more passed before he realized he was looking at the wrong bank. He turned in the water, arms and legs pumping, and saw it.

The tree seemed impossibly distant. Miles away. In reality, it was only about a hundred feet away. But as nearly exhausted as he was from his efforts to battle the current and stay afloat, those hundred feet might well have been a thousand.

A wave slammed into his face, and he was forced to swallow water. He began to sputter—and to sink. He kicked rhythmically again, wishing he could free his feet of the waterlogged boots which were weighing him down as if they were bricks that had been tied to his feet. He managed to stay afloat and to begin to swim back upstream toward the cedar which offered him at least a chance, however slim, of getting out of the river and away from the distinct possibility of being swept over the waterfall to his death.

Head down, body knifing through the water with his legs hanging down because of his waterlogged boots, he swam on, lifting his head every few seconds to gulp down air which did nothing to soothe his burning lungs. He kept at it, arms flailing, his will to survive a frantic drumbeat in his mind and heart.

He made progress, although he paid a steep price for that progress in terms of aching muscles and a heart strained to the bursting point. He was, he estimated, only twenty feet from the cedar when an overwhelming weakness swept over him. All at once it seemed as if he could not lift his arms anymore. He wanted to stop, to drift, to catch his breath and wait for the pounding of the blood in his tortured brain to stop. A part of him knew that if he dared to obey the perverse and potentially deadly impulse that had seized him, he was doomed.

Fighting against the urge to give in and let the river have its way with him, he swam on. He refused to think about the pain in his lungs or the weakness that was draining him of everything but one final burst of energy and effort as he continued struggling to stay alive.

Suddenly, a gray mist rose up in front of him. At first, he thought it was spray from the turbulent river. But then he knew it was not as the mist deepened in color, turning from gray to black.

He couldn't see! He was losing consciousness!

Panic seized him. When he felt himself sinking, that panic grew in size and strength. He heard a scream, a cry for help, and it was not until many seconds had passed that he realized it had come from his own throat. The sound had been torn from him, a desperate cry from a drowning man.

The blackness abruptly dissipated and the wet world into which he had fallen came once again into sharp focus. Gabe cursed the water. He cursed the cougar that had been responsible for him being where he was.

A loud report disrupted his thoughts and silenced his curses which had emerged from his lips as little more than faint sighs. The sound slowly penetrated his consciousness, and he realized with a certain bemused surprise that what he had just heard had been a gunshot.

A gunshot? Who had fired it? From where? He looked around. At first, he could see no one. But then a second shot sounded, and he turned his head and saw a man and a buckskin horse standing high up on the bank of the river between the cedar tree that had been his destination and his present position in the river.

He raised a hand and feebly waved to the man who seemed to be watching him. He tried to call out, to shout for help, but all he could manage was a hoarse croak.

The man responded, but the sound of his words was drowned out by the roar of the river. He held up one hand, palm outward and facing Gabe, who continued struggling to reach the bank, as if to ask him to wait.

I can't wait, Gabe thought with a mixture of anger and dread. Can't you see I'm about to drown, dammit!

The man on the bank took a coiled lariat from his saddle horn and began to unwind it. He stepped up to the edge of the bank, whirled the end of his lariat above his head, and then let it fly.

Gabe's eyes never left the lariat as it snaked out above the surface of the river in his direction. He stopped dog-paddling, almost stopped breathing in the clutch of his growing anxiety as he reached up with both hands to seize the rope.

It hit the water with a splash about four feet from where he was. He lunged for it, but the river, in an almost playful way, whirled it away from him. He was vaguely conscious of the man on the bank yelling something to him as he fought to grab the floating rope. He reached for it, but it eluded him as the river's current took control of it. Then, incredibly, the rope was withdrawn. He turned his head and through the veil of river water that was dripping from his hair and forehead into his eyes he saw the man on the bank reeling in his lariat.

A strangled cry escaped his lips. His hands reached out in a helpless gesture as the lariat was drawn out of the river. He moaned. He felt himself sinking. He tried again to swim, but he had next to no energy left for such a trying task. He lay back in the water and let himself float, let himself be toyed with by the river, trying to think of nothing, certainly not of death by drowning. . . .

His eyes began to close. Then they snapped open—wide open. The lariat was soaring over his head. Then it dropped down, striking him in the face. He almost wept with relief as he seized the rope and silently thanked the man on the bank for his second on-target toss of the lariat.

He clutched the rope tightly in both wet hands and almost immediately felt himself being drawn toward the bank. His legs hung down deep into the water because of his waterlogged boots but that no longer mattered. All that mattered was the man on the bank who was now in the saddle of his buckskin with the other end of the lariat dallied around his saddle horn.

Gabe sucked air into his lungs as the man backed up his horse, pulling on the lariat. As the buckskin continued backing up under the guidance of its rider, the lariat remained taut and Gabe drew closer and closer to the shore and safety.

He had almost reached it when his left hand lost its grip on the rope and his right hand nearly did the same. He frantically grabbed it more tightly and held on, his knuckles turning white with his effort.

"Hold on!" yelled the man who was hauling him ashore.

This time Gabe was close enough to hear his encouraging words despite the sound of the river that was reverberating in his ears.

He held on. Tightly. As if he would never ever let go of the rope that was the only link between him and life. When his tightly clenched hands first touched the mud of the riverbank, he wanted to whoop with joy. But he found he could not make a single sound because he could barely breathe.

His rescuer on the bank above him hopped down out of the saddle. His buckskin remained where it was, keeping the lariat taut. The man scrambled down the slippery slope of the shore and grabbed both of Gabe's hands in his, which proved to be impressively strong. He dragged Gabe up the bank through the mud that splattered both of them. When he had Gabe safely ashore, he released his hold on him and straightened up.

Gabe found himself staring up into a pair of bright blue eyes set in a round face notable for its rosy cheeks and dimpled chin. The man looming above him had skin that had been sunburned. Gabe estimated his age at somewhere between twenty and twenty-five. Neither short nor tall but of average height, his body looked as strong as his hands had just proved to be.

Gabe tried to match his rescuer's smile but what he managed was a lopsided effort at best.

"That was a bath that ought to last you a lifetime," the man said jovially, his smile broadening. "What happened, mister? It's not Saturday night and yet where did I find you? Right in the middle of the biggest bathtub this side of the Missouri River."

Gabe tried to answer the question, but he couldn't seem to get his vocal chords to work properly.

"You okay, are you?"

Was he? A little the worse for wear he wanted to say but could only gasp and sputter as his lungs continued to burn.

"Is that your gray I ran across back aways?" the man asked him.

Gabe managed a feeble nod.

"That rifle and dead sheep too?"

Gabe nodded again.

"I'll go get them for you. I reckon there's no use me telling you to stay put. You don't look to me like you can do much else but stay put, the condition you're in."

Gabe remained where he was on the muddy ground. He folded his arms and laid his head down upon them.

The next thing he knew he was being shaken. Only then did he realize that he had been asleep for a while. He raised his head and opened his eyes to see his rescuer leaning down over him and shaking him by the shoulder.

"That's no place to take a nap. I'll take you back to my camp. You can sleep there if you want to. Can you ride?"

Gabe wasn't sure whether he could or not. He made up his mind to try. He started to get to his feet but faltered and slipped back down to the ground. His companion helped him rise. Gabe stood there, leaning against the man for support and wishing he could regain the strength he had before his long battle with the river.

"Over this way." The man helped him walk to his gray. Once there, he boosted Gabe into the saddle, stepped back, and gave him a sober look. "You think you can stay up there?"

Gabe, as if in answer to the question, began to sway in the saddle. He reached for his saddle horn, missed it, tried again to grab it, and again it eluded him.

"Sit tight for a minute. I'll fix you up fine. It'll only take a minute or two."

The man disappeared. When he returned he was carrying his lariat. He proceeded to cut two lengths of rope from it. He bent down and reached under Gabe's horse as if he intended to tighten Gabe's cinch. But that was not what he had in mind. Minutes later, Gabe's ankles were tied together beneath the barrel of his gelding. Minutes after that, his wrists were roped to his saddle horn.

"I reckon we're ready to move out now," the man announced, apparently satisfied with what he had just done. "By the way, my name's Purcell. Oscar Purcell. I wish it was just plain John or James or something simple like that even though those monikers do sound sort of solemn and biblical-like. But my parents stuck me with Oscar. Don't have the least notion why they had it in for me."

Oscar's guffaw was merry and bright, and Gabe was glad to be alive to hear it. He wanted to tell the man so, but before he could, he fell asleep in the saddle as they moved out, heading for Oscar's camp.

Gabe smelled something. Something sweet and tantalizing. His nostrils twitched. Consciousness gradually returned to him. He opened his eyes and looked around. Daylight. Dawn, to be exact about it. Dawn? How long had he slept? A day? Longer? He propped himself up on his elbows and saw Oscar Purcell hunkered down with his back to him in front of a campfire he was diligently tending. That was where that appetizing smell was coming from. But with Oscar in the way, Gabe could not see what he was cooking.

He turned his head and saw Oscar's buckskin browsing nearby. Not far away was a mule wearing a halter attached to an iron picket pin driven into the ground. Between the mule and the fire was a jumble of boxes and gunnysacks.

Looking back at Oscar, Gabe sniffed the aromatic air and decided he could guess what the man was cooking. He was roasting bighorn sheep.

When Oscar turned toward him, Gabe saw that he was right. Through Oscar's parted legs, which formed an inverted V, as he stood smiling down at him, Gabe could see a haunch of the sheep he had shot spitted over the fire and dripping fat into it as it cooked. His mouth watered.

"Welcome back to the land of the living," Oscar greeted him.

"How long—"

"Have you been asleep? Since yesterday when we got back here. Did anybody ever tell you, you snore like a buzz saw?"

Gabe grinned.

"You got yourself a name, have you?"

"It's Conrad. Gabe Conrad."

"Glad to meet you, Gabe Conrad. You remember my name? Oscar Purcell?"

"I remember. I want to tell you I'm much obliged to you, Oscar, for saving my life like you did."

"Glad to have happened along when I did. It was the damnedest thing, I can tell you."

What was? Gabe wondered.

Oscar continued. "There I was riding along minding my own business and there he was. Your gray. Standing there a'munching some chokecherry bushes like he hadn't a care in the world, never mind a master. Next thing I seen was a rifle lying on the ground. After that, the carcass of a shot bighorn. Now that's funny, says I to myself. Where do you suppose the fellow is who rides that gray and shoots a bighorn and then throws his rifle away like he regrets what he's gone and done?"

"It wasn't like that—"

"I scouted the ground. Found some sign. Cat tracks. Boot tracks. Followed them up the slope of that limestone hill back where we met. Saw you bobbing around down there in the river like a cork somebody had thrown in, by gum. What the hell happened to you, Gabe?"

"A cougar happened to me. At least, that was the start of what happened to me. I shot the bighorn, but then the cougar showed up and seemed to think that the sheep was his kill since, I gather, he'd been tracking it same as me. Well, we had us a bit of a set-to since I wasn't about to give up the sheep without a fight and neither, as it turned out, was he. It ended up with the pair of us falling head over heels into that river you dragged me out of."

"What happened to the cougar?"

"He went over the waterfall."

"You'd best wash out that wound on the back of your hand there. It looks a sight, and if it gets infected, it could turn nasty on you."

Gabe looked down at his clawed hand. "You know, at one point I thought for sure I'd killed that cat. He didn't move when I booted him. I made the bad mistake of turning my back on him, and he came after me. I reckon he was knocked out, not killed like I thought at the time. That's when the two of us wound up in the drink."

"Well, it's over now. You're here and the cougar's not. Thank heaven for small favors, is what I always say."

Gabe glanced at the creek that flowed through a grove of pine trees not far from the campsite. "Is there time for me to wash up before that meat's cooked?"

"Sure there is. Plenty of time. It takes awhile to roast that haunch clear through, though I prefer it with the blood still oozing out of it myself. How about you?"

"Any way at all's fine and dandy with me. I'm so hungry right now I reckon I could eat it raw."

Gabe got to his feet and, moving slowly since he quickly discovered that muscles he never knew he had had stiffened on him, made his way to the creek. There he stripped and proceeded to wash himself in the clear cold water, paying particular attention to his clawed hand. He used sand to scrape the grime and mud from his body and face. When he was finished, he dried himself with handfuls of grass he plucked from the ground. His clothes were still damp from the river, but he put them on anyway, giving the tear in his sheepskin jacket a rueful glance.

Oscar, seeing him glance at the torn jacket, remarked, "A man needs a woman out here in the wilderness for sewing rips like the one you've got and for a few other things I could mention but, being the shy man that I am, I won't, lessen it bring a blush to my cheeks. Say, your hand looks worse now than it did before."

"That's because I scraped away the dried blood to let it bleed again and clean itself out. That's an old Indian trick I learned somewhere along the trails I've been riding."

"Where you from originally?"

Gabe hesitated as he always did when someone—particularly a white person—asked him about his origins. He was reluctant to discuss his boyhood with the Oglala with such a person. There were far too many Indian-haters around and, although he doubted that Oscar Purcell numbered himself among them, he had decided long ago that some stones were better left unturned.

"Me, I'm from Ohio originally," Oscar volunteered when Gabe did not immediately respond to the question. "I was born on a hardscrabble farm there, me and my six brothers and sisters. But somewhere along the line I got a hankering to go westering and westering I went and here I am, as you can plainly see. Well, I'd best turn that spit so the meat'll brown up nice and even."

Gabe watched Oscar as he hunkered down and turned the spit. The smell of the roasting meat tantalized him and caused his gut to begin to grumble.

"You're a hungry man it sounds like," Oscar observed.

"I am that." Gabe thought of the last time he had eaten. The great burdock plants he had consumed had not held his hunger at bay for very long. He licked his lips as he eyed the meat turning on Oscar's spit, and saliva flooded his mouth.

Later, when the meat was thoroughly cooked, the two men ate, cutting pieces from the haunch with their knives and impaling them on branches.

"This here's real tasty," Oscar commented, wiping grease from his lips and chin with the back of one hand. "Juicy. Just the way I like it."

Gabe nodded as he chewed and swallowed a crusty piece of meat. He promptly cut another one for himself.

"Which way you headed?" Oscar asked him. "East or west?"

"I was headed east when I met up with that cougar."

Oscar studied him for a moment and then, when Gabe said no more, he let the matter drop. He filled two tin cups with coffee from the pot which sat in the fire and handed one of them to Gabe.

"It's strong," he warned. "That's about all I can say for it. It's strong enough to stand a spoon straight up in it, as a matter of fact."

"The way I like it." Gabe drank, washing down the meat he was devouring. He nodded in the direction of the pack mule. "You're not exactly traveling light," he observed.

"That's true enough," Oscar cheerfully agreed. He pointed to his mule. "Old Mehitabel over there, she's been protesting darn near every step of the way since we left Sacramento."

"Sacramento, huh? That's where you hail from?"

"It is. It's not a bad town. I miss it sometimes. It and the girl I left behind me back there."

Gabe smiled as he continued eating.

"Her name's Molly Hastings. She's a true vision of loveliness is my Molly. She's an angel. She even sounds like one. She certainly looks like one. Sometimes when I'm with her, I feel like I don't deserve the great fortune the good Lord's seen fit to bestow upon me."

"It's none of my business, Oscar, but I'm wondering why you're out here and the love of your life is back in Sacramento."

"No surprise you're wondering, considering the way I've just been raving about my Molly. You've got every right in the world to wonder whether I might not be touched in the head to up and leave her behind in trade for this mountain wilderness where a man could get himself killed as quick as a cat laps sweet cream. But I've got a good reason for being where I am."

Oscar gave Gabe an appraising look and then busied himself tearing chunks of meat from the large piece he had impaled on the branch. He chewed thoughtfully, glancing at Gabe from time to time as if he were trying to make up his mind about something.

Finally, he said, "You want to know what it is, my reason for being here in the middle of nowhere?"

"I tend to respect other men's privacy, Oscar. Why you're out here—that's none of my business."

"You're right on that score. But I'm going to tell you anyway. It's a secret, sort of. Which is funny when you come right down to think on it since there's hardly another soul out here to tell it to, which sort of makes it something other than a secret, don't it?"

Gabe wondered what Oscar was getting at as the man laughed heartily at his own words.

"I'm out here prospecting," Oscar finally declared and watched Gabe closely for his reaction to the announcement.

Gabe avoided looking at him as he said, "Lots of men have prospected in these mountains. But I kind of thought that all that activity had more or less died down since the gold rush back in the early fifties."

"Well, you're right. Not many men prospect for gold these days. Things are pretty much played out in the gold fields. Sutter's Mill—these days, it's not even much of a tourist attraction. The American River's a quiet place now that's been pretty much taken over by the birds and beasts that were there before everybody and his brother went there to see the elephant, as they used to say. But what I'm doing, it's altogether different."

"How different, if you don't mind my asking?"

Oscar hesitated, and Gabe could tell that he was wondering if he had revealed too much already and was having second thoughts about going on.

A moment later, Oscar seemed to throw caution to the wind as he said, "I'm after a treasure that may be as rich as any King Croesus ever dreamed of."

"Oh?"

"It's gold, of course. It's in a lake somewheres up here in the hills. A lost lake. That's where the gold is."

Gabe suppressed a groan. He had heard countless fanciful tales of lost lakes of gold. Of hidden caches of gold that some enterprising slicker was selling maps to with the promise that anyone who followed his map would soon be richer than he had ever dared hope to be. Gabe could never understand why, if such a person's maps were reliable and to be trusted, their proprietor didn't use them himself to find the lost gold and be done with it.

"The Indians who used to live around here," Oscar continued, "knew about the lost lake. In fact, I've got a map right here." He pulled a folded piece of dirty paper from his vest pocket and handed it to Gabe.

Gabe took it, unfolded it, and scanned it.

"It's not the clearest map in the world or the easiest to follow, but it'll have to do me until something better comes along," Oscar commented with a smile.

"I take it you've not tracked down this lost lake of yours yet."

"Nope. Not yet. But I will. You can bet your best boots I will. Someday. Someday soon, I hope."

Gabe handed back the map. "You been looking long?"

Oscar lowered his head. He gnawed his lower lip while a muscle in his jaw jumped. "Weeks," he finally said in an almost inaudible voice. "Almost a month, to tell the truth."

"No luck, huh?"

Oscar shook his head.

"Well, places change, you know. Take these mountains, for example. There are landslides. There are storms that blow trees down that have been landmarks on a man's map. All sorts of things happen to change the face of the land. Which tends to make it hard to find what a man's looking for, never mind that he's got himself a map that points him the way to it."

"Right you are. I tell you, I've been traipsing all over God's grand domain these past weary weeks, and I haven't turned up a thing except any number of what turned out to be false trails. Oh, I found some gold dust in some rocks I ran across two weeks ago, but it weren't nothing worth writing home about. Nowheres near to the bonanza that's said to be in the lost lake I'm out here hunting."

Gabe started to say something, but Oscar hurried on as if to forestall him. "Don't get me wrong. I'm not discouraged. Not much, anyway. I mean to keep at it until I find that lake and the gold that's in it."

"You're sure it's there? You really believe there is a lost lake?"

Oscar looked at Gabe as if he had just doused him with a bucketful of cold water. His lower jaw dropped. His blue eyes seemed to darken. "Do I believe there is a lost lake? Why, sure I do. Gabe, don't you see? I *got* to believe in that lake. It's my one big chance to get rich and make Molly the queen she truly deserves to be. This may be my only chance to strike it rich. A chance like this doesn't come down the pike every day of a man's life. Not this man's life, at any rate."

Gabe's eyes were on Oscar as he sat hunkered down beside the fire, his food forgotten, his eyes aglow with visions of lost lakes full of bright beckoning gold.

"Look at me," Oscar said dolefully. "I'm nothing, that's what I am. I told you I was from a family of farmers in Ohio. Now I ain't saying there's anything wrong with farmers or farming. Hell, man, they're the salt of the earth, farmers are. But the point I'm making here is that I had high hopes of being something a whole lot more than just a clodhopper the rest of my born days. Not at first, you understand. But I did after I met up with my darling, Molly. That's when things changed for me. You could say she inspired me. Yep, that's exactly what she did—she inspired me to make something special out of myself. Well, sir, I asked myself, now how am I going to do a thing like that? A thing like that, that's quite a trick to turn if you take my meaning.

"Well, I pondered on it. I soon found out to my everlasting shame that I had about as much chance of making something special out of myself as a fort in a tailwind. I mean, I only got through the third grade in our one-room schoolhouse back in Ohio. I can do sums if the arithmetic don't involve real big numbers, and I can read if the book in question don't contain real big words. But what's all that amount to? Even stagecoach robbers can do those things fairly well, some of them, I hear.

"No, I came to see my problem just as plain as day. My problem, I came to understand, was that I didn't have no special thing about me, not in body and not in mind and not in soul, that was going to boost me head and shoulders above the fellas in any kind of crowd. So I was stymied, you see. There I was in love with Molly and what did the future hold for us?

"Then, the Lord be praised, I ran into this drunken Indian back in Sacramento, and he spilled the beans about the lost lake of gold the Indians of his outfit knew all about. I guess what I did was I took advantage of that old son. Like I said, he was drunk as a deacon, so I pumped him for information and he talked. Oh my, didn't he just! When he was finished, I tell you I saw sugarplums made of gold dancing in front of my dazzled eyes."

Oscar suddenly grew solemn. He frowned at Gabe. "I made up my mind right then and there that I was going to find the lost lake. I told the Indian I'd pay him fifty dollars to take me to it. Of course, I lied. I didn't have but two dollars between me and the poorhouse. The Indian, he said he was too old to go traipsing about through the Sierra Nevada Mountains. But, he said, he'd draw me a map from memory. His daddy, he said, had taken him to the lost lake when he was a boy and showed it to him in all its golden wonder. He still remembered how to get there, he said.

"He wanted my fifty dollars for the map. I had to tell him the truth then. That I only had two dollars and— as it ended up when I turned all my pockets out—four cents in change.

" 'I'll take it,' he said without batting an eye. 'You can pay me the rest when you find color up in the mountains.' He drew the map, and I paid him two dollars and four cents for it. He went his way—into the saloon— and I went mine. With a map worth a million dollars in my pocket."

Oscar beamed at Gabe.

Gabe lowered his eyes to avoid revealing what he was thinking about the Indian and what he was sure was a bogus map, not to mention a bogus story about a lost lake of gold.

"That drunken Indian," Oscar continued, "he told me how the lake of gold got to be the way it is. What he said was, he said that the lake was situated right in the middle of his tribe's stamping grounds, and it had a big old serpent down in it. Now that serpent, the old son said, got fed once a year. I'll bet you can't guess what it was fed with, can you?"

"Gold."

"Well, in a manner of speaking, yes," a disappointed Oscar said. Then, brightening, he added, "The gold— let me step back a bit and start over. Every year at the appointed time, the medicine man of the tribe, he chose the finest specimen of young manhood he could find among the braves. That fella was going to be fed to the serpent so it wouldn't raise hell and havoc with the Indians.

"What they did then, the Indians, was they coated this fella they'd picked out with pitch, then they sprinkled him all over with gold dust, then they put him in a canoe and they rowed him out onto the lake and tossed him in it so the serpent could eat him up. That's how the gold got in the lake."

Still Gabe said nothing. He didn't ask where the gold had come from that the Indians used to coat their sacrificial victim with. He didn't ask why the serpent only ate once a year—and then ate the flower of the tribe's young manhood.

"I reckon I must be going about this hunt the wrong way," Oscar said, his head hanging down again. "I must be doing something wrong or I would have found that lake and all the gold in it by now."

Gabe tried to push the idea that had just occurred to him out of his mind. But it wouldn't go. After all, Oscar Purcell had saved his life. He owed the man something, didn't he? He was in Oscar's debt. And it had become perfectly clear to him now how he could go about trying to repay that debt as he listened to his companion. But it was all nonsense. And yet . . .

He turned the thought over and over in his mind, examining it from every angle. What did he have to lose? Nothing, he decided. He had nowhere to go or be at any particular time. So why not?

"You know what they say, Oscar," he remarked.

Oscar looked at him. "What do you mean? What do they say?"

"That two heads are better than one."

Oscar frowned, studying Gabe as if he were a puzzle he had stumbled upon. Then his eyes widened, his lips parted, and he began to smile.

"Do you mean to say that you—that you and me—"

"We might do as a team what you've not yet been able to do by yourself. Namely, find the lost lake of gold."

Oscar shot to his feet. He took off his hat and threw it high into the air. He did a little dance, accompanied by whoops of pure delight, around the fire. Then he halted and happily held out his hand to Gabe.

"Shake, partner," he said, smiling broadly. "If we find any gold, we'll split it fifty-fifty. Fair enough?"

"Fair enough," Gabe said, although he knew he would never see a grain of gold while engaged in repaying Oscar Purcell for having saved his life.

CHAPTER THREE

Gabe awoke early the next morning to find that Oscar was already up and cooking breakfast.

"I figured on getting an early start," he told Gabe, who sat up, shook out his boots, and pulled them on. "The early bird gets the worm, or so they say."

Gabe folded his bedroll and rose. He poured himself a cup of coffee and drank it hunkered down beside the campfire that shed welcome heat to dissipate the chill of the misty mountain morning.

"I'll ride out, too," Gabe offered, the coffee warming him as he drank it.

Oscar gave him a skeptical look. "Maybe you ought to rest for another day or two. You had yourself a pretty rough time in that river."

"I'm feeling fit and itchy to be on the go again."

"Well, you know best, I reckon. I planned to head east today. It's about the only direction left that I haven't already scoured in my hunt for the lost lake."

"You've been out that way, have you?" Gabe asked, pointing across the fire's flickering flames to a range of mountains off to the north.

"Yep. Twice. No luck either time."

"I'll take a crack at it."

"But, like I said, I scoured every inch of that range and found no lost lake or anything else worth mentioning neither."

"Maybe you might have overlooked something."

Oscar shrugged. "Suit yourself. But, if you ask me, you're just wasting your time. What made you decide to head off in that direction anyhow?"

"That map of yours did. As I recollect, it showed a pair of peaks as one of the landmarks on the way to the lost lake. And there's a pair off yonder." Gabe pointed to the peaks that loomed side by side like two stern sentinels in the misty distance.

"You mind if I ask you something?"

"Ask away."

"Yesterday when I showed you the map I got from that tipsy Indian back in Sacramento, you didn't seem all that excited by it. I got the impression then—correct me if I'm wrong—that you didn't think it was worth all that much."

"I didn't say that."

"You didn't have to. I could see you were thinking it."

"I'm not one to look a gift horse in the mouth." Gabe paused long enough to empty his cup and then refill it. "Unless it turns out to be nothing more than crow bait, the horse I mentioned. So far as I'm concerned, your map hasn't proved itself to be no good. So I thought the smartest thing I could do would be to take it serious. And the only landmark I can see that also appears on the map is those twin peaks. So I decided to head there—for starters anyway."

"Breakfast's about ready. There's potatoes baking in the coals, and that pot's got some sheep stewing in it. Help yourself."

Gabe did so, and the two men ate in silence that was broken only by the sound of an oriole singing its small heart out as it greeted the dawning day.

When the remains of the meal had been cleared and the fire stomped out, Oscar said, "By the way, Gabe, I stuck your hat on your saddle horn and your rifle in your saddle scabbard."

"I saw it when I came round yesterday morning."

"You sure don't miss much, do you?"

"I try hard not to. What a man misses might be the making of the end of him."

Oscar nodded thoughtfully.

"You mind if I take another gander at that map of yours before I move out?" Gabe asked him.

Oscar pulled the map from his pocket and handed it to Gabe who unfolded it and studied it carefully.

There were the twin peaks he noted, carefully drawn with pencil on part of the map. There was also a tall tree— it was impossible to tell what kind of tree it was from the drawing—and a scrawl in one corner that looked like nothing Gabe could recognize. It was bisected by a wavy line that ran off the bottom of the paper and stopped dead in the middle of it. Not much to go on. Maybe nothing to go on. Maybe the map was truly nothing more than a figment of the besotted imagination of the Indian who had drawn it for Oscar. But Gabe had decided to give it the benefit of the very large doubt he harbored concerning its authenticity and head in the direction of the pair of peaks which were the map's dominant feature.

"I notice there's no X that marks the spot on this thing," he remarked, indicating the map in his hand.

"Which doesn't help us at all, does it?" Oscar asked ruefully. "I noticed that same thing after I'd started out, but when I went back to town to find that Indian who sold me the map, it turned out he was long since gone."

"You mind if I keep this map with me while we go on the scout today, Oscar?"

"You're welcome to it. I know it by heart anyhow."

Half an hour later, both men rode out, Oscar heading east, Gabe heading north.

Gabe had not gone far when he crossed a narrow stream that bubbled along the side of a low hill. He smiled at the sight of an ouzel that was busily hunting its breakfast. The bird, about the size of a wren with a gray body and a white breast, walked, as was its strange custom, along the bed of the stream, its head bobbing as it tried to dredge up a meal—insect larvae that clung to the bottom of wet rocks which the bird easily overturned.

As he passed the ouzel, it dived into the middle of the stream and began to walk underwater along its bottom as it continued poking about for food, the scaly trapdoors over each of its nostrils tightly closed to allow it the luxury of its odd underwater excursion. A moment later, the ouzel was not walking; it was flying upstream— underwater!

Farther along, where the stream widened and deepened, Gabe was able to make out the flash of several golden trout which were disporting themselves in the icy water. One broke the surface to gleam in the sunlight before falling back into the water and continuing its journey.

The mountain air warmed as the mist slowly dissipated, burned off by the sun. Gabe kept his eyes on the peaks and the land surrounding them as he rode on. The peaks were, from time to time, wreathed in wispy white clouds as a result of their elevation. At other times, the sun glinted on their caps of snow, causing them to gleam as if someone were sending signals from them.

They were, he found, more distant than he had initially estimated. It was mid-afternoon by the time he reached the foothills leading up to them. He rode through the underbrush growing at the base of the peaks and, when he was halfway up to their summit, he halted. Sitting his saddle, his hands folded around his saddle horn, he surveyed the land below him.

He saw no sign of any lake.

But that did not disappoint him. The map was, after all, crudely drawn and, as he had mentioned to Oscar earlier, it gave no indication of the precise location of the lost lake—if such a lake did indeed exist. Or had existed. He peered through the remains of the mist drifting through the valley below him as he searched for signs of a dry lake bed. Lakes had, he knew, been known to dry up over a period of years. Maybe the one he was searching for had done just that. But no dry lake basin was visible anywhere in the area.

He turned his gray and rode to the northwest, circling below the peaks above him. Later, after completely circling the mountain, he still had seen no sign of a lake anywhere in the vicinity. He took Oscar's map from his pocket and studied it again.

A squiggly line going nowhere and possessing no meaning that he could comprehend. A tree. And the two peaks. He returned the map to his pocket, rode down the mountain, and spent the rest of the day riding through the surrounding mountains—particularly through a heavily forested area where he might have missed seeing a lake from the summit he had climbed. No luck.

He dismounted long enough to pluck some leaves from some dandelions growing in a meadow. He chewed them as he traveled onward through thick growths of weeds, the sweet scent of cedar in his nostrils.

Overhead a hawk soared, riding the wind currents. Gabe watched it swoop down and then rise again with a California ground squirrel thrashing helplessly in its talons.

He was on his way back to camp late that afternoon when he found himself crossing the same stream he had forded earlier in the day. He glanced back at the peaks that had been of no help to him in his hunt as he rode on. The snow on their summits now glowed orange which soon faded to purple as the sun sank behind the mountains.

"Any luck?" a hopeful Oscar called out to him as he rode into camp that night.

"None," he answered.

The firelight playing across Oscar's face gave him the look of an imp. A disappointed imp. "Well, tomorrow's another day. You hungry?"

"As a bear."

"Light and cool your saddle. Supper'll be ready in two shakes of lamb's tail."

It was. It consisted of more sheep—boiled again and seasoned with salt.

After the meal, Oscar lit a pipe and blew smoke rings into the night. He kept up a cheerful conversation about nothing in particular but before long his voice trailed away.

Gabe, his back braced against the trunk of a sequoia, knew the man was discouraged. It was apparent in the way Oscar's shoulders slumped and the corners of his mouth drooped.

"Maybe I should pack it in," he said after a long silence. "Maybe there just ain't no such thing as a lost lake." He looked up at Gabe, who wondered if Oscar wanted him to deny his speculation. If so, Gabe was not about to do so. He himself had little belief in Oscar's story of the golden lake or in the map Oscar had bought that was supposed to point him in the direction of El Dorado.

Oscar lowered his head, seemingly unaware that his pipe had gone out. "I think I'll turn in," he said and got to his feet.

Minutes later, he was wrapped in a blanket not far from the fire but, Gabe suspected, not asleep judging by the way he tossed and turned.

Gabe looked up at the starry sky where the air was

not haunted by dreams of gold. Above him the wind moved through the branches of the trees like a ghost moaning about its lost life. In his mind, he could see the twin peaks he had visited earlier during the day. The stream that was home to the golden trout. The squiggly line drawn on the map which went nowhere. And the tree that might have been any one of a hundred trees he had passed that day. None of it made any sense to him. But, as Oscar had said, tomorrow was another day and maybe then, maybe tomorrow, one or the other of them would find what was Oscar's heart's desire—the lost lake of gold.

Neither of them found the lake the next day. Or the day after. Or the day after that.

A week after meeting Gabe, Oscar finally announced that he was calling it quits.

"I'm throwing in the towel," he declared over a supper of stewed mutton and wild turnips. "I've traipsed up hill and down dale in these damned mountains until I know every rock and rill by their first names. I've been on a wild-goose chase, no two ways around it. I'm heading back to Sacramento come morning."

"Well, you gave it your best try," Gabe pointed out in an attempt to console the doleful Oscar who was staring moodily into the fire. "A man can't do much more than that."

"A man damn well *can* do more than that!" Oscar snapped, almost snarling at Gabe. "He can *succeed* in what he sets out to do, *that's* what more he can do. I damn well *didn't*!"

"I know you tried, but sometimes things just don't work out the way a man wants them to."

"She'll hate me," Oscar moaned. "Molly'll say I'm a failure."

"Not if she really loves you, she won't. She'll understand you did all you could."

"I started a feed and grain business back in Sacramento," Oscar said. "I only lasted two months before I went bankrupt. After that I tried trading horses, and I didn't have the head for that neither. I got cheated right and left and wound up losing every cent I'd put into the string I started with. Molly, she'll see this venture as just one more failure on my part. I mean, how long can a man expect a woman to put up with somebody like me who can't make a go of anything he turns his hand to? She's got a right to want nice things. A settled life. A secure one. When I go back this time and tell her I failed again, she's going to think at least twice before she'll consider hitching her wagon to my horse. Any woman with half a brain in her head would. I don't blame her, you understand. I reckon I'd do much the same thing were I in her place."

"Some men just take longer than others to find out what it is they're skilled at," Gabe offered. "You're one of them, it appears. But if I were you, I wouldn't be so hard on myself. Something'll turn up and work out, you'll see."

"Fat chance," Oscar snorted derisively.

"Let's give it one more try," Gabe suggested. "Let's you and me ride out together tomorrow. Maybe as a team we can find that lost lake since neither one of us has been able to come up with it on our own. What do you say, Oscar? One more try?"

Oscar frowned.

Gabe gave him an encouraging smile.

"Alright," he said at last. "One more try. Which way do you want to go?"

"Let's scout the twin peaks area again."

"Gabe, I've been there more than once already, and you've been there, too, and there's no lost lake anywhere over that way."

"But there's golden trout," Gabe pointed out. "Big fat beauties they are, too. I saw them in a stream when I rode that way. We could get a real early start tomorrow morning, and we could catch some of those fish for our breakfast. Doesn't that proposal make your mouth water like the river Jordan though?"

Oscar managed a weak smile. He pointed to the pot containing the stewed mutton. "To tell you the truth, I've about had me a bellyful of salted sheep. Trout would be a tasty change."

They broke camp the following morning by the light of their fire and were on their way to the twin peaks area before the first gray light of false dawn streaked the sky, Oscar trailing his pack mule and Gabe dreaming of the sweet taste of trout.

When they reached the stream that had been their destination, they dismounted, and Gabe used his knife to cut a thin branch from a cedar sapling which he whittled into a makeshift spear. He took up a position on the western bank of the stream so that he would not cast a shadow on the water once the sun rose. Such a shadow, he knew from experience, would frighten away the fish.

He stood on the bank while Oscar removed some of the gear from his pack mule and began to build a cook fire.

"Am I right in starting a fire?" Oscar asked, "or am I just some kind of cockeyed optimist?"

"I fully expect to catch us some breakfast," Gabe assured him, "so I reckon you're right in wallowing in optimism."

A flash of color beneath the surface of the water attracted Gabe's attention. He bent over and saw a golden trout, its body weaving as it swam downstream. He raised his spear, took aim—and missed the fish which went speeding through the water and out of sight around a bend.

"You missed," Oscar said as he joined Gabe on the

bank. "I'm starting to turn pessimistic."

Gabe watched the water. Crayfish darted about the silty bottom, their tails propelling their movements. Minnows like silver threads stitched the stream. He saw no more trout.

Minutes passed.

The two men watched the water as they waited, the smoke from Oscar's fire drifting upward into the sky.

"There's one!" Oscar cried, pointing to the water.

Gabe didn't see any trout. "Where?" he asked.

"Right there. It's as plain as the nose on your face. *There!*"

"That's not—" Gabe began as he saw the glint of color that Oscar was pointing at so excitedly. "That's—"

What was it? He thought he knew. He hoped he was right. He knew it was no trout. It didn't move. But, as the light of the rising sun which was still partially hidden behind the mountain peaks flickered on the running water, the color glittered, faded, and glittered again.

"What are you doing?" Oscar asked in mild exasperation as Gabe dropped the spear in his hand and strode into the rushing water. "You'll scare the fish."

Gabe bent over and reached below the surface of the water. He came up with a handful of silt mixed with sand from which he plucked a young crayfish and threw it away. As the material he had scooped from the bottom of the stream oozed through his fingers, he found what he had expected to find. Flakes of gold were mixed with the worthless debris. He turned and held out his hand to Oscar as the water flowed across his boots and his feet began to get cold.

Oscar looked down at his hand and then up at him. "What—"

"Look real close."

Oscar bent his head and did as he was told. "I don't see—" Then he raised his head and stared at Gabe. "Is it—"

"It is."

"Gold!" Oscar shouted, and the word came echoing back from the mountain range.

Oscar was laughing as the contents of Gabe's out-stretched hand slipped away to fall back into the water. Then he was bending over and scrambling along the bottom of the stream, bending over and coming up with handfuls of silt and sand—and an occasional flake of gold. His laughter grew louder and tears appeared in his eyes.

"This sure ain't no lake," he laughed, his voice crack-ing, "but it sure as hell *is* gold we've found! I'll go get my pan, and we'll get to work getting it out of here," he exclaimed, excitement sharpening his voice and brightening his eyes. He started up the bank to where his mule was browsing the bark of a yellow pine. "Ain't you coming?" he called back to Gabe.

"You go ahead and start panning," Gabe answered as he stepped out of the water and began walking upstream, his breakfast forgotten, his mind on more important things.

He heard Oscar call out to him, but the man's words were whipped away by the wind and he didn't hear them. Rounding a bend, his eyes on the stream, he saw more color. Color that was not the gold of a school of golden trout which were feeding in the stream.

He looked up. The stream wound its way up the side of the mountain. A hundred feet from where he stood, it vanished. Gabe quickened his pace and soon reached the spot where the stream had seemed to vanish into thin air. Or, rather, into the basalt side of the mountain which formed a sheer wall that prevented Gabe from going any farther. He hurriedly pulled aside the tangled undergrowth at the foot of the basalt slab and found the entrance to a cave from which the stream emerged to flow down the side of the mountain.

Holding the undergrowth aside, he peered into the

interior of the underground cavern but could see nothing. He could only hear the rush of water and the sound of water dripping coming from the darkness within. He let go of the bushes and stepped back. He looked around for a moment and then went over to a sycamore that was growing not far from the cave's entrance and broke off a branch. He gathered some pitch from a nearby pine tree and smeared it on one end of his branch to turn it into a torch. He took a wooden match from a metal container in his pocket and lit the torch.

Then, pulling aside the undergrowth again, he stooped and entered the cave. Letting the underbrush fall into place behind him, he moved deeper into the cavern, following the course of the stream. Stepping around stalagmites that thrust upward from the uneven dirt floor of the place and ducking stalactites that hung from the curved ceiling, he made his way through a tunnel-like passage which, after a time, widened into a vast cavern.

Here the stalactites hung high above his head. Here the stream had its origin in an elongated lake that bubbled noisily in its center, a sound that testified to the underground springs which had created the lake and the runoff from it which formed the stream that flowed out of the cavern and down the mountainside.

When Gabe reached the lake's shore, he began to circle it. He lowered his torch in order to see down into its murky depths. Visibility was poor, but he managed to make out craggy outcrops below the water's surface. He caught a brief glimpse of an unrecognizable species of albino fish which was obviously blind since there were thick scales covering the shallow sockets where its eyes should have been.

He walked on slowly as he continued examining the rock formations just below the surface of the water. He had begun to think the theory he had formulated when he first saw the traces of gold in the stream outside had been wrong. But then he came upon a ledge that jutted out into the lake, a ledge located about a foot below the surface of the body of water. Excitement surged through him. He got down on one knee and lowered the torch even more so that it was almost touching the water.

What he had thought he had seen was actually there. A gold quartz vein ran through the ledge of rock. Gabe estimated its length at nearly five feet. It was, as far as he could tell by the weak light of his torch, a good foot high. The precious metal glinted as the surface of the water shifted slightly from a faint breeze that came from an unseen source.

"Gabe!"

The sound of his name being called by Oscar Purcell reached him, but just barely. The sound was faint, seeming to come from another world. And it had come from another world, he thought. It had come from that sunlit world outside the cavern which was so unlike the stygian one in which he found himself. He turned and hurried back toward the entrance to the underground chamber. When he reached the narrow tunnel, he lowered his head and made his way toward the faint glimmer of light at its far end.

"Gabe, where are you?"

He began to run, his flaming torch casting huge fluttering shadows on the damp walls as he did so. He burst out of the cavern and into the light of the sun which was above the mountains now and which made him squint and blink until his eyes became accustomed to its brightness.

"What were you doing in there?" Oscar asked him.

"Looking for a lost lake of gold."

"When you didn't come back . . ." Oscar's words faded away. Then, "What did you say?"

Gabe repeated what he had said.

Oscar smirked. "Did you find a lost lake of gold in that hidey-hole behind you?"

Gabe nodded.

Oscar's lips worked, but no words emerged from his mouth. He pointed at the now hidden entrance to the cavern, a questioning expression on his face.

Gabe nodded again.

"You found—" Oscar managed to croak but was unable to say any more.

"I found your lost lake of gold," Gabe told him. "When we found color in the water downstream, I had a notion that it must have been washed downstream from somewhere up here in the mountains. So I set out to see where the stream started."

He turned and pointed at the basalt wall. "It starts in there. There's an underground spring that's created a big lake in that mountain. The stream's the runoff from that lake."

"The gold—"

"It's under the water. Not very far under. Easy to get at if a man doesn't mind standing in water to work it."

"Did you see—was there any sign of the serpent that eats men in the lake?"

"Nope, not a one. The closest thing I saw to a man-eating serpent was a blind white fish that was swimming around in the lake."

"This couldn't be the lost lake the Indian told me about. He never said it was underground."

"Maybe it's not that lake," Gabe said. "On the other hand, it might very well be. That Indian of yours might have gotten things a mite mixed up. On the other hand, that squiggly line on your map—now I realize it was meant to be the stream that flows out of the mountain."

"But the Indian, he never said nothing about the lost lake being under the ground."

"From what you told me, he also never said it wasn't, did he?"

"That's true enough. He didn't." Oscar took a step forward. "I'm going in there. I want to see the gold with my very own eyes."

"You'll need a torch if you're to do that. It's as black as Satan's heart inside there."

It took only a few minutes to make a torch for Oscar, and then both men shoved the underbrush aside and, with Gabe leading the way, they made their way through the cavern to the location of the bonanza Gabe had discovered.

"How much farther is it?" Oscar asked when they had gone no more than a few yards.

"My, oh, my," Gabe declared, expressing mock exasperation, "you sure are an impatient son."

Their voices echoed in the dark vault that was full of shadows thrown by the flames of their torches and thick with the smoke those torches gave off.

Then the smoke dissipated as they emerged from the narrow tunnel into the huge chamber where the lake lay.

Oscar took one look around and then glanced at Gabe. "I don't see any gold."

Gabe got down on one knee and held his torch over the surface of the lake. "Look."

Oscar knelt down beside him and peered into the depths of the lake. At first, he apparently saw nothing. But then, his lower jaw dropping, he muttered an awed oath.

"It's really true," he breathed as he stared at the vein of quartz that was shot through with gold. "Look at it, Gabe! There must be a fortune in gold in that rock!"

"Now the trick is to get it out of there," Gabe said.

CHAPTER FOUR

In the days that followed, Gabe and Oscar worked from dawn to dusk getting the gold out of the lake. They used picks while standing in the cold water to dislodge the rock. Then they shoveled it into buckets, the bottoms of which they had pierced to allow the lake water to drain out of them, and carried the buckets up onto the shore. There they used hammers to pound the rock, chipping away the quartz until only malleable lumps of gold remained. They wrapped the gold in tarpaulins and stored it in the cavern so that, should anyone happen upon their camp outside, there would be no evidence of what they were doing in the vicinity.

On the third night following their daylong labors in the underground vault, they finished their supper and sat beside the fire as Oscar smoked his pipe and talked of the future and of dreams that come true.

"In my heart of hearts," he said at one point, "I think I never really did believe that there was a lost lake. In my heart of hearts, I think I thought I was off on a fool's errand. But, by golly, I wasn't! Isn't that a remarkable thing though?"

"We've just about got out all the gold there is to be

gotten out of there," Gabe observed.

"Enough to make us both rich for the rest of our natural lives. Isn't *that* a remarkable thing, too?"

Gabe said nothing as he continued to stare into the fire.

"Molly is going to be thrilled to death when I get back home and tell her we're going to be living the good life, her and me. She'll probably faint at the first sight of the gold when I show it to her. But it won't be long before she gets used to having more money than she rightly knows what to do with.

"And as for me, I'm going to buy myself a fancy suit and a silk cravat to go with it, and you know what else? Spats. I'm going to buy myself a pair of fancy spats. I've always had a hankering for a pair of spats. They're the mark of a real gentleman, you know. I'll put on my new duds, and once I'm all dolled up, I'll take Molly by the arm—she'll be wearing a dress of silk with little seed pearls sewed onto it here, there, and everywhere—and we'll take ourselves a stroll through downtown Sacramento. We'll stop traffic and scare horses, I reckon.

"Everybody'll be giving us looks like they never did see anybody so fine and fancy as the two of us. They'll be asking themselves who the two swells are. We'll just sashay right on by like we've both been born with silver spoons in our mouths and all this commotion is something we got used to a long, long time ago.

"Oh, there's a great day coming. I can see it all now, and I can tell you, Gabe, my good friend, I *like* what I see!"

"I'm going to turn in," Gabe responded. "Tomorrow's another day."

"Tell me something, Gabe. What are you going to do when we're all finished up here?"

"Mosey on."

"I've been thinking. Maybe you'd consider coming

back to Sacramento with me. I could introduce you to Molly. I know she'd be mighty pleased to meet the man who made me rich."

"I'm not much of a city man," Gabe said. "I tend to like the open country where a man can be free and easy. Towns and cities, they make me feel like I'm walking on eggs when I'm in them."

"You wouldn't have to stay. You could, you know, just visit for a spell."

Gabe shook his head.

Oscar muttered an oath. "The way this old world of ours turns, it's enough sometimes to make a man's head swim. Here I go and make a good friend, and the first thing you know I'm going in one direction and he's headed off in another one."

"If I ever get to Sacramento, I'll look you up, Oscar. You and Molly Hastings."

Oscar looked up at Gabe, his eyes brightening. "You will? You really will?"

"That's a promise. One I'll keep. Count on it."

They had finished gathering the last of the gold an hour after the next day's dawn, earlier than either of them had expected to complete their labors.

"Well, I reckon it's time to divvy up the booty," an expansive Oscar declared when they had gathered the gold into the center of a tarpaulin spread on the ground.

"There's no divvying up to be done, Oscar. The gold's yours."

"Hey, now, hold on, my friend. This gold's as much yours as it is mine. I told you when you said you'd pitch in and help me hunt for it that we'd split whatever we found right down the middle. I'm a man of my word, Gabe. That's what I intend to do."

"I don't mean to make you mad, Oscar, but I don't want any of that gold. You did most of the work looking for it—"

"But *I* didn't find it. *You* did."

"Be that as it may, the gold's yours. As was the map. As was the information you got from that Indian about the lost lake. I lent you a hand in the hunt for it because I figured I owed you at least that much for pulling me out of the river and saving my life. Now, the way I see things, the record's been set straight. So let's wish each other luck and part good friends. What do you say?"

"I say you're a strange fellow, that's for certain, Gabe. Most other men, if they'd latched onto an opportunity like this, would be more than happy to take fifty percent of the gold. Some might even have been willing to cut my throat and take the whole kit and caboodle and never mind half of it. You're sure you won't change your mind?"

"I'm sure. You have yourself a safe journey back to civilization, hear? Watch out for any desperate characters you might meet who might take a notion to prey on an innocent fella such as yourself who's all alone out here in the wilderness."

"Nobody'll bother me."

"I was joshing, of course. But you were pretty open and aboveboard with me when we first met about what you were up to out here—about the gold and all. Sad to say, that may not be the best policy for a man in your present position to follow. I just thought I'd offer you what I consider to be a word of advice."

"I appreciate your concern, I really do. Remember now, I'm holding you to your promise to come visit Molly and me in Sacramento if you ever find yourself in our neck of the woods."

Gabe held out his hand.

Oscar took it and shook. He started to say something but then turned away and began to fill a gunnysack with his gold.

Gabe went over to his gelding. He flipped his stirrups up onto his saddle, hunkered down, and tightened his cinch. Then he flipped his stirrups down and stepped into the saddle.

When Oscar looked up at him, he gave the man a wave and rode out.

A magpie chattered above him in the branches of a tree, and somewhere off in the distance a loon called. Lonely sounds. But they didn't bother him. He was a man accustomed to being alone. At times he preferred being alone. Those times when he didn't, those times when loneliness lay heavy on his heart, he kept himself busy or went in search of companionship—usually female—and the loneliness passed. For a time.

The chattering of the magpie faded away into silence as did the demented cry of the loon. Gabe rode on, his feet out of the stirrups, his hands easy on the reins. He headed east, the direction in which he had been traveling when he had had the good fortune to be rescued from the river by Oscar Purcell.

Thinking of the man and the relatively brief time they had spent together, he found himself envying his friend. Oscar had a woman he loved, and now he also had a fortune. Those facts added up to just about all that was needed to make a man not just content but downright happy in white society. He hoped Oscar knew that he was a mighty lucky man.

He ducked to avoid a low-hanging branch of a pine tree and then turned his horse to circle around a pile of rocks that lay directly in his path. The rising sun was not yet in sight, but soon it would be and then, before long, it would be boiling. Hot days and chilly nights; that was the way things were in the Sierra Nevada Mountains, even in the spring. Not until full summer did the nights even approach being balmy. Then they—

Gabe suddenly drew rein. Stiffly, he sat his saddle, all his senses alert. He had heard the sound of a shot. It had come from behind him. He glanced over his shoulder but saw nothing and had known he would see nothing. The shot had come from too far away.

He thought of Oscar Purcell. He thought of Oscar Purcell's gold. He turned his horse and slammed his heels into it. As the gray went galloping back the way they had come, Gabe found himself hoping the shot he had heard had been made by no one more harmful than a hunter. But a tense feeling was twisting his gut and an ugly premonition was unsettling his mind.

He slowed his horse as he approached the area from which he believed the shot had come. His eyes roamed through the trees, up a wooded hill, down into a dry gulch, and across a rocky expanse of ground. He saw no one. He heard nothing.

Wait . . .

He did hear something. The sound of a branch snapping. Where? Up ahead of him. The sound was coming from a dense stand of timber. From the very spot where he had so recently parted company with Oscar Purcell.

He stood up in his stirrups, drawing his rifle from its saddle scabbard as he did so. He brought the gun up to his shoulder, his eyes on the trees. His finger tightened on the trigger, drawing it slowly back, as he saw someone moving in the trees.

Time stopped.

A man appeared among the trees, half-hidden by them as he moved from one to another as if counting them. The man touched a trunk, moved on, touched another trunk, moved on.

No, he was not touching the trunks. He was placing his hands against them. He was using them as supports.

Gabe's eyes narrowed as he dropped back down into the saddle. The man looked like—

It *was!* Oscar Purcell!

Gabe spurred his gray and moved toward the fortune hunter. He ducked under low-hanging branches as he went, his rifle now cradled in the crook of his arm.

Oscar emerged from the trees into plain sight. He

stood there staring at the approaching Gabe, his eyes wide and his mouth open. His arms were thrust out in front of him as if he were reaching for something or someone. He halted. His lips worked, but no words emerged from them.

"Oscar," Gabe said, his voice sounding loud in the surrounding silence. "You alright, Oscar?" Then he saw the neat red hole in his friend's chest and knew he was not alright.

Oscar took a step forward and then another one. His arms still reaching and his lips still working, he pitched forward and fell facedown on the ground.

Gabe slid out of the saddle and, carrying his rifle, hurried over to Oscar. When he reached him, he dropped down on one knee beside his friend. It was then that he saw the large ragged hole in the man's back that had torn both flesh and shirt. He looked up and quickly scanned the area. He saw nothing and no one. Whoever it was who had shot Oscar was now nowhere in sight. But, Gabe knew, that did not mean the person was not nearby. Perhaps lurking among the trees. Waiting to kill two birds instead of just one.

Gabe realized as he formed the thought in his mind that he knew Oscar, though still alive, was a dead man. No man could survive the wound he had suffered. Gabe found it incredible that Oscar had managed to walk following the round that had torn into his chest and out his back. The round which may well have torn apart his heart and one of his lungs in its fiery passage.

"Gabe . . ."

Gabe bent down low to hear Oscar's whispered words as the man turned his head to one side and stared blankly at him.

"The gold . . ."

When Oscar said no more, his lips working uselessly, Gabe asked the question that was in his mind and to which he thought he knew the answer. "What about the gold, Oscar?"

"Gone."

The word seemed to toll like a somber bell in the quiet landscape. It seemed to turn the world dark.

"Gone," Oscar managed to repeat. "The gold." A bloody froth bubbled up and out of his mouth to stain his chin and throat.

"What happened?"

Oscar's eyes held Gabe prisoner as they continued to stare at him. "Somebody . . . shot me."

"Who?"

"Didn't . . . see who. Must have passed . . . out. When I came to . . . my gold . . . gone." The bloody froth turned into a wet stream and poured from Oscar's mouth, making him cough and close his eyes in horror and agony. Then, after a long moment during which he gagged and choked and shuddered violently as if a cold wind had caught him in its clutches, he managed to murmur, "Get it, Gabe."

Gabe frowned.

"My gold. Get it back for me, Gabe. Get it—give it to Molly. Can't do it myself. I'm . . . a goner. Know it."

Incredibly, Oscar laughed, a cracked sound in the stillness.

Gabe gripped his friend's arm as Oscar began to tremble and then to shake.

"They say," Oscar continued, his eyes still shut and his fingers feebly clawing the ground, "that up here . . . is the air . . . the angels breathe. Sweet mountain air. Makes a man giddy."

Oscar coughed. Gouts of dark blood flew from his mouth.

"Take it easy, my friend," Gabe said, feeling powerless, unable to think of anything that could ease his friend's pain or hold at bay the death that was so determinedly stalking him.

"Will . . . will you do it?"

Gabe answered without a moment's thought or hesitation. "I'll do my best to get your gold back from whoever stole it from you. You can count on me to do that, Oscar, if I possibly can."

"You'll give it to Molly when you do?"

If I do, Gabe thought, but he said, "I will, Oscar."

As if Gabe's words were all he had been waiting to hear, Oscar's fingers stopped scrabbling along the ground. His eyes eased open, and he almost smiled. "Knew you wouldn't . . . let me down."

Gabe lowered his head in sorrow as Oscar's eyes darkened in death.

Gabe placed a final stone atop the grave he had dug for Oscar and stepped back. He took off his hat, bowed his head, and said a silent prayer to *Wakan-tanka,* the Great Spirit. He prayed that, even though Oscar did not bear on his forehead the blue dot or on his chin the two tattooed lines which would prevent *Hihan Kara,* the Owl Maker, from forcing Oscar's soul off the Ghost Road in the sky as it traveled to the Hereafter, that Oscar would nevertheless reach his destination safely.

Then he began the next task he had set for himself once the burying and praying were over. He began to search for sign of the person who had murdered his friend. His search began with him standing beside the new grave topped with stones and slowly turning in a tightly circumscribed circle. His eyes roved about the area. They noted the droop of tree branches, the condition of the grasses growing in the area, the way rocks lay on the ground.

After a few minutes of this, he began to walk about, again in a circle, this one widening as he continued his search for sign. He found the spot where Oscar had been shot. Blood spattered the ground there. On that ground lay a spent shell. Boot prints, unclear but very definitely present in the dust, could be seen near the shell.

Gabe followed them. They led him away from Oscar's campsite and into the woods. They eventually led him to a spot where a horse had browsed the bark of a tree to which it had been tethered. The horse had restlessly torn up the ground while it awaited the return of its rider.

Gabe studied the trail horse and rider had left when they departed the area. Then he returned to the campsite and his gray. Moments later, he was back in the saddle, leading Oscar's buckskin and his pack mule, riding out after the man who had murdered his friend.

A kind of spine-tingling thrill coursed through him as he rode, his eyes on the ground. His blood flowed fast and hot now that he was once again a hunter. Not for food this time but for blood vengeance. And something more as well. The return of the gold that had been stolen from Oscar along with his life.

The hair on the back of his neck stood up in anticipation of what was to come—the finding and punishing of the prey he was now trailing, whoever that might turn out to be.

He spurred his gelding as the trail revealed that the person who had killed Oscar was traveling fast. The leather of the reins wrapped around Gabe's hand felt hot, and there was a burning sensation in his body that came not from the sun that was now in sight above the mountain peaks but from the boiling hate within him. The hate he had for whoever had ended Oscar's life and taken his gold.

Sometime later, he crested a hill which was lined with slender lodgepole pines whose scent sweetened the air, and he saw, far below him in a sheltered valley that was rich with grass, wood, and water, nearly a score of circled Conestoga wagons. From his vantage point, he could see that the trail he had been following led down the hill and in among the wagons.

He clucked to his gray, and the horse, front feet stiffly braced for the steep descent, made its way slowly down the hill. He halted his horse at the bottom of the hill and stepped down from the saddle. He hunkered down, his eyes on the livestock, horses and oxen, which he could see in the center of the circle made by the wagons which were interlocked, the tongue of one extending under the wheels of the one next to it.

He saw a man appear at the rear of one of the wagons and jump down to the ground. The man looked around somewhat stealthily, Gabe thought, and then, seeing no one, sprinted toward a wagon some distance away into which he promptly disappeared.

"Whatcha doin'?"

He had heard the young girl approaching from the side and had seen her out of the corner of his eye. "Nothing much," he answered. "Yourself?"

"Same as you. Nothin' much."

"You're out for an early morning stroll, I take it."

Her answer was a sly smile.

She was, Gabe estimated, not much more than six-teen—seventeen at the outside. Built as solidly as a four-seater outhouse with big firm breasts and hips that looked like they could comfort a man were he to lay himself down between the girl's long lean legs. Her hair was the color of sunstruck wheat and her lips were, in the words of a woman he had once known, "bee stung." Which meant plump and pouty. She had big brown eyes that would have done credit to a fox.

"I had to answer a call of nature," she told Gabe as she boldly watched him watching her.

He said nothing.

"I ain't seen you around before. You fixin' to join our wagon train?"

"I might."

"If you do, you'll be about the best-lookin' feller we got amongst us, and that's a true fact."

Gabe suppressed a smile.

"My name's Ada Murdoch. What's yours?"

"Gabe Conrad."

From within the circle of wagons came the sounds of people moving about. Fires were being built and breakfasts cooked over them. Men had begun hitching their livestock to their wagons.

The smell of food cooking drifted in the air. Someone cursed a recalcitrant cow that did not want to be milked although its udder was filled to bursting. The cow responded by kicking over the stool of the would-be milker.

"We're California-bound," Ada announced, drawing a nondescript pattern in the dust with the scuffed toe of one high-button shoe. "It seems like we ain't never going to get there, though. We've been on the trail for ever so long, and California's not nowheres near in sight as of yet."

She stared into the distance, a wistful expression on her pretty face as she shielded her eyes from the sun with one hand.

"That there's the man in charge of us," she volunteered a moment later. She pointed to a burly man with a full red beard and eyes as blue as cornflowers who was shouting directions to the wagon drivers as they got their wagons ready to roll. "His name's Ed Brock, and he makes me mad the way he's always givin' orders. 'Do this and do that,' is what he's always sayin' until a body sure enuff gets mighty tired of his big mouth and the way he uses it. He'd make some woman an unhappy wife, if he up and married her."

When Gabe said nothing but continued to study Ada—her half-childlike and half-womanly face and her ripe body, she added, "Me, I'm not never going to get married. I'm going to have me a good time and not get trapped into bearing babies and having to put up with all the other awfulness that goes along with *that* sorry task."

"Have you got a beau, Ada?" Gabe asked in a neutral tone of voice, but his eyes were sparkling.

She stood in a provocative stance, one arm folded across her flat belly and the other propped up on it with an index finger touching her dimpled chin. "What do you think?"

"I think the boys would be standing in line to walk out with you of an evening, that's what I think."

Ada laughed. "You think right, Gabe. You don't mind if I call you by your given name, do you?"

"I don't mind one bit."

"The boys—the men, too—they come a'sniffin' round me like a pack of woebegone hounds, they do. It gets tiresome at times."

"Ada, get yourself on in here and see to breakfast, you hear me, gal?"

Gabe's head turned to the side as Ada snorted and muttered something under her breath. He saw a short fat man with a bullwhip standing between two of the wagons, glaring at Ada.

"That there's my pa," she declared. "He's worse than Mr. Brock if the truth's to be told. Well, I gotta go. It's been nice meetin' you, Gabe. If you should decide to hook up with us, you come round and say howdy to me once you get settled in, hear?"

"I'll be sure to do that, Ada."

"Gal, get you in here, and I mean right now!" Murdoch bellowed.

Ada groaned theatrically and started toward her father. She tossed Gabe a backward glance. And a come-hither smile.

But he walked instead toward Ed Brock, leaving his horse and Oscar's stock to graze the bluestem that covered most of the floor of the valley.

"Mr. Brock," he said, after stepping over the upraised tongue of one of the wagons, "my name's Gabe Conrad, and I would like a word with you."

"Glad to meet you, Conrad," Brock said, taking Gabe's hand and shaking it. "What's on your mind?"

"Murder, Mr. Brock."

Brock's eyes widened. He spat a brown stream of tobacco juice on the ground by his boots. "You don't say?"

"I do say."

"Who got murdered and why, if you don't mind me asking?"

"To answer your first question, it was a man named Oscar Purcell who got himself shot to death by somebody. Oscar was a friend of mine. As for your second question, whoever shot him did it to get their hands on Oscar's gold that he had with him."

"Gold, you say," Brock declared thoughtfully as he worked his chaw from one side of his mouth to the other. "Guns and gold—they make for a potent mix."

"So my friend, Oscar, found out to his everlasting sorrow."

"Got another question for you, Conrad."

"Ask it."

"What's your friend's death got to do with these two score and six souls I'm shepherding to California?"

"Maybe nothing. But I've got my suspicions that whoever it was did in Oscar is probably amongst the folk you're taking west."

Brock's eyes narrowed as he studied Gabe. "You accusing me or one of mine?"

Gabe shook his head. "Nope. I'm just saying I have reason to suspect that the murderer might be with your outfit."

"What makes you think that?"

"I found sign. Followed a trail that led away from Oscar's camp. The trail headed straight here."

"People ride out of here for one reason or another. Some for romantic reasons, if you follow me. Or just to get off by their lonesome and away from being packed cheek to jowl with a whole lot of other people. Then they ride back. That doesn't mean—"

"I thought I might ride along with you," Gabe interrupted.

"You got any money?"

"No."

Brock shook his head, squinting into the sun. "Well, you may or may not know it, but in a company like this one"—he waved his hand in a gesture that encompassed the wagons and the people they belonged to—"each and every family or individual traveler pays a fee to belong to the company. I have to ask you to pay or you'll have to ride on alone. To let you join for free, that wouldn't be right. Wouldn't be fair to the rest. I think you see what I'm getting at."

Gabe said nothing for a moment. Then, "Maybe I could work for the right to ride along with you all."

"Got all the able-bodied men I need, Conrad."

"Ed!" a man suddenly shouted. He was standing in the distance beside a lone wagon that had been separated from its neighbors. "Ed, look!" He pointed to a pair of oxen lying on the ground, their bellies bloated.

"Well, I'll be damned!" Brock exclaimed, pulling his hat down low on his forehead. "That Henry Ferguson can get himself in more goddamned trouble than three pups in a basket."

Brock strode away from Gabe, heading for Ferguson and his oxen.

Gabe followed him. He joined Brock and Ferguson in time to hear Ferguson lament, "It must have been the water in that hole we passed yesterday."

"Of *course* it was the water!" Brock bellowed. "I told you—I told everybody—not to let their stock drink any of that damned water!"

"My oxen were on their last legs," Ferguson explained as he seemed to wilt under Brock's fiery stare. "They needed water bad. They weren't about to last lessen I let them drink."

"Well, you can kiss those oxen of yours good-bye,

Ferguson," Brock said flatly. He reached out with a boot and nudged one of the oxen. It didn't respond. Its eyes remained closed as its belly heaved and a greenish froth emerged from between its lips. "That water they drunk, it was alkali-charged."

Several people had gathered nearby to listen to the conversation between Brock and Ferguson. They had looks of pity mixed with fear on their faces as their gazes shifted from Ferguson to his oxen and then back to Ferguson again. They knew, Gabe realized, the bleak prospects facing Ferguson if his oxen died and he had no replacements for them.

Gabe had seen trails littered with abandoned wagons, household goods, and sometimes even provisions. Beside them often lay the sun-bleached bones of oxen or mules which all bore mute testimony to the fact that some emigrants, upon the death of their stock, had been forced to travel on foot carrying the little they could as they continued their westward journey. Sometimes, farther on, he had come upon graves bearing crude wooden markers with names and dates carved upon them, indicating that the owners of the oxen had followed their stock down into death.

He caught a glimpse of Ada Murdoch among the people watching the scene. He moved over to where she was standing and spoke softly to her.

She nodded and walked away. Gabe followed her.

When he returned a few minutes later, he was carrying a clear glass bottle stoppered with a cork. The bottle contained a colorless liquid.

"Brock," he said, "maybe I can help Mr. Ferguson out of the ditch he's in."

All eyes turned on him, Brock's and Ferguson's among them.

Ada Murdoch, who had returned with Gabe, said, "Mr. Conrad thinks he can cure Mr. Ferguson's cattle."

"You can't cure alkali-poisoned stock," Brock pontificated. "They're goners, both of them."

"Sir, if there's something you can do," Ferguson ventured, addressing Gabe, "me and my family'd be much obliged to you."

Gabe ignored Brock. He knelt down next to the pair of oxen.

"What's in that bottle?" Gabe heard a male voice ask from behind him. He glanced over his shoulder and answered, "Vinegar."

The man who had spoken to him had a familiar face. Gabe had seen it soon after he arrived at the camp. The man who had just questioned him was the one he had seen emerge from one of the wagons and then disappear inside another one.

He was a thin man, more bone than flesh. His cheeks were sunken beneath sharp cheekbones, and his black eyes seemed to recede into his head beneath the craggy overhang of his broad brow. There was an odd handsomeness about him that had its roots in his leanness and was enhanced by a kind of sultriness present in the glow of his black eyes and the fullness of his lips. He wore tight jeans and highly polished boots. His hat, a Stetson, had a curved brim that shadowed his face and gave him a certain air of jauntiness.

"That's George Gordon," Brock volunteered from behind Gabe as Gabe forced open the jaws of one of the oxen and poured a liberal dose of vinegar down the animal's throat. The beast coughed violently and tossed its great head.

"Howdy," Gabe said to Gordon without looking up from what he was doing.

Gordon didn't respond.

Gabe administered the same treatment to the other ox. Both of them tried to rise, but both failed to do so, slumping weakly back down on the ground. Another dose of vinegar brought the same response—coughing and a futile attempt to rise.

Gabe got up, corked the bottle, and handed it to Ada.

She took it from him as if it had been a priceless gift, her adoring eyes fastened on him as she clutched the bottle in both hands.

Gabe addressed Ferguson. "Have your missus give them another dose of vinegar, if she's got any, in about an hour," he advised.

"If Missus Ferguson is out of vinegar," Ada said, "she can borrow this." She held up her bottle.

Ferguson acknowledged her offer with a nod. To Gabe, he said, "Will that stuff do my animals any good, do you think?"

"I've seen it work wonders in cases of alkali poisoning," Gabe replied. "But just to help things along some, ask your wife to fry up some bacon and force it down your animals' throats. The bacon and vinegar together just might do the trick."

"Are you a doctor, Mr.—" George Gordon inquired, letting his question trail away.

"The name's Gabe Conrad," Gabe said. "No, I'm not a doctor."

"I'd like a word with you, Conrad," Brock interrupted rather brusquely, "but it'll have to wait. We've got to get moving. You can stay with the train if you've a mind to."

"I told you I don't have any—"

"You just keep your mouth shut and stay with the train," Brock interrupted. "A man who's got tricks like dosing poisoned stock with vinegar and bacon, he might could come in handy along the trail. Besides which, like I said, I want to talk to you about what we were discussin' a little bit ago."

"You mean the murder?"

"What's this about a murder?" Gordon asked, his brow furrowing.

"It's a private matter," Brock told him bluntly. "A personal matter. Hadn't you folks best be about hitting the trail?"

The people began to move away to the wagons, George Gordon among them.

"My wife, Liza," Ferguson said to Gabe, "she'll be real pleased to learn you fixed our ailing oxen for us. She for sure wouldn't relish walking the rest of the way to California, though I reckon my two young sons might think it was some kind of adventure." He smiled wanly.

Ada took Gabe's hand and led him away from the wagons as Brock shouted orders and the emigrants busied themselves getting their wagons ready to roll.

"You'd best get ready to move on, hadn't you?" Gabe asked Ada as she led him through the tall grass toward a grove of trees growing in the distance. "You and your daddy don't want to be left behind."

"I'm not in no particular hurry," Ada responded. "Not to hit the trail, I'm not," she added with a meaningful glance at Gabe. "There's other things though I could be said to be in a hurry over."

Other things?

Moments after they had entered the shady grove where they could no longer be seen by anyone in the camp, he found out what Ada was in a hurry for as she put down her bottle of vinegar, threw her arms around his neck, and kissed him full on the lips, her hot tongue forcing its way into his mouth.

CHAPTER FIVE

Later, as Ada pulled her dress back on over her head and wiggled her ripe body to smooth it into place, she said, "We'd best not be seen together, so I'll go on back first. You come along a little later."

"You don't want your daddy to see us together, is that it?" Gabe said, buttoning his shirt.

"He's a mean man. He don't hold with a girl like me pleasuring herself like we just done."

Gabe watched Ada as she walked out of the grove, her hips swaying, her hair bouncing lightly on her shoulders. He finished dressing, pulled on his boots, and stood up. Above him, a crow cawed as it flew through the air. He began to pace. When at last he decided enough time had passed, he went to the edge of the grove and peered out.

Most of the wagons were on the trail. Some remained behind as their owners lingered over their breakfasts. Henry Ferguson's wagon was one of them. However, the reason for his delay was not a lazy breakfast but the illness of his oxen, one of which, Gabe was pleased to note, was now up on its feet. He saw no sign of Ada. He did see Ed Brock aboard his horse vigorously waving the wagons along as he led the way west.

He left the grove and returned to his horse. Swinging into the saddle and leading Purcell's horse and mule, he took up a position at the end of the train.

Dust swirled through the air, churned up by hooves and wagon wheels. Some of the dust found its way into Gabe's mouth and nostrils. He untied the bandanna he wore around his neck and used it as a mask in the fashion favored by road agents in an effort to block the dust. His ploy was only partially successful. Some dust still found its way into his nose which caused him to cough from time to time. Behind him, Purcell's mule brayed and balked. He jerked the rope that encircled its neck and, after putting up a brief fight, the mule gave in and plodded on.

When Gabe passed the Ferguson family, Henry waved to him and said something to the woman who was frying bacon over their cook fire as he pointed at Gabe. The woman gave Gabe a smile.

He touched the brim of his hat to her. The two little boys at the woman's side stared shyly at Gabe. When his gaze fell on them, they looked everywhere but at him. Mrs. Ferguson was busily engaged in feeding the oxen pieces of crisp bacon as he left them behind.

A young man with eyes and hair the color of acorns and a ready smile rode up beside Gabe.

"Howdy," he said, offering his hand. "I'm Hal Slade."

"Gabe Conrad."

When the two men had shaken hands, Slade said, "I guess we're the only two loners in this outfit, which means we're outnumbered by family groups. I'm glad you hooked up with us. People have been looking askance at me ever since I joined the train, like as if there's something sinful about being a single man."

When Gabe made no comment, Slade continued, "That was a neat trick you pulled with Mr. Ferguson's oxen. They're on the mend now. Ought to be as good as new pretty soon from the looks of them."

"I'm glad to hear it."

"What you fixing to do once you get to California?"

"Hard to say. I'll wait and see what turns up, I reckon."

"I'm going to get me a homestead. Not a big one. Not at first. I don't have a whole lot of money, so I'll have to start small. But in time I hope to have a nice spread. I hear growing fruit is big business out in California. I might be a fruit farmer. In time I'll find me a wife and we'll have young'uns, and the first thing you know, I'll be first or second cousin to prosperous, I'll bet."

"I wish you luck."

"I wish you the same, Mr. Conrad."

"Where you from?" Gabe asked Slade, keeping his eyes straight ahead.

"Massachusetts. I joined up with this outfit in Independence, Missouri. I always have had a hankering to see California. On top of that, I decided to take old Horace Greeley's advice. You probably know what he's supposed to have said. 'Go west, young man, go west.' Well, I'm going."

The smile on Slade's face grew, and he seemed to bubble with excitement mixed with a healthy dose of youthful enthusiasm. He fidgeted in his saddle, his hands clasping his saddle horn and then letting it go to make a sweeping gesture. His eyebrows rose and fell like a barometer gone wild.

Gabe found himself liking the young man and envying his ebullience which was a characteristic of the young, he thought. They—the young—met the world with a laugh and a hearty embrace. The young had nothing to fear, or so they believed. The world was their oyster. It held no terrors for them because their few years were usually, as yet, empty of disaster and of disaster's twin, grief.

"How much longer do you reckon it'll take us to get to where we're going?" Slade asked.

"Hard to say. If the going turns out to be easy, it shouldn't be more than a few more days. But if it turns hard, it could take a lot longer."

"Hard?"

"There've been known to be bad snowstorms in the mountains this time of year. Then there's floods which cause the rivers to rise, and that makes fording them a ticklish business. That sort of thing can slow us down."

"We've already had our share of troubles. Like what happened to Ferguson's oxen which, most folk figure, was his own fault for letting them drink where they had no business being. Missus Lane, she lost her man back along the trail. He just sickened up and died on her. Nobody knows why exactly. She's pretty cut up about losing him. One family we had with us threw in the towel when we were only five days out of Independence. They just couldn't take it, it seems. It'd been raining for days. The womenfolk had to hold up umbrellas when they cooked. Some of the wagon covers leaked. It was no picnic, I can tell you. So this family I'm talking about, they decided one day they'd had enough, and they just turned around and headed back to Missouri."

"The people on the train, how are they, generally speaking? Peaceable people? They get along good together?"

"Well, I can't speak for anyone but myself when you come right down to it but, yeah, I'd say most of the people on the train are fine folk."

"Most of them," Gabe prodded.

"There's some raise a fuss or shirk their share of the work. Like Jack Murdoch. He had a fight with Ed Brock the other day. A real knuckle-and-skull affair it was, too. I never did find out what it was all about. Neither man would say. But Mr. Murdoch, he like to have killed Mr. Brock, he did. I never did see a man with such a pure look of hate on him before as he had for our wagon master."

So there was at least one man—maybe two men—capable of violence connected with the train, Gabe silently mused.

"But most of the folk," Slade continued, "are just plain quiet people. God-fearing, most of them. Ready to lend a hand to a neighbor without being asked. Like Mr. Gordon."

"George Gordon? I met him soon after I arrived." But he seems to have more than one roost, Gabe thought to himself. Ducks out of one wagon in the dawn's early light and right smack into another one. Which makes a man wonder what he's up to.

"Mr. Gordon," Slade offered, "has been an aid and comfort to the Widow Lane ever since her man died. Mr. Gordon sometimes leaves the driving of his wagon to his wife and goes and drives the widow's for her. Just to give her some respite. The widow's sorrowing over her loss has taken a toll on her."

"Gordon sounds like a decent enough fellow."

"He is. Of course, that ain't to say he's some kind of saint."

Now what, Gabe wondered, did Slade mean by that remark? He wasn't long in finding out.

"There's been talk," Slade said. "Folk say Mr. Gordon has a roving eye and it roves from his wife to—so some whisper—Gwen Landon. But no man's all good all the time, I say. It wouldn't be natural. A man has to sow his wild oats, and some—like Mr. Gordon, if the whispers are to be believed— make damn good sowers."

Slade laughed lightly. "I myself say more power to Mr. Gordon if he can win the ladies like some say he does. In fact, I envy men like him. I wish I could be more like them. But I'm not handsome and I'm not smart so the girls don't exactly come crowding around me. They can tell after one look at me and after hearing me open my ignorant mouth that I'm not the pick of the Slade litter by a long shot."

"How old are you, son?"

"Sixteen, going on seventeen. Why?"

"Just wondered. You've not got your full growth yet. With a little luck, you might turn out to be a veritable Romeo when you get to be a little older and maybe a little wiser in the strange ways of women."

Slade glanced at Gabe, his cheeks flushing. "You think so? Do you really?"

"It's been known to happen."

"Did it happen with you?"

Did it? Gabe decided a kindly lie was in order. "It did. When I was your age—that's some time ago, you understand—I was bandy-legged and skinny as a snake. Had the looks of a kicked cur and the courage of a mouse. The years have sort of smoothed things out some for me and the ladies—well, now, they don't turn and run anymore when they see me coming."

"You're not a bad-looking fellow," Slade observed, eyeing Gabe. "It's hard to believe you were what you said you once were. Not to look at you now, I mean."

"So keep your chin up and don't despair, son. If I could turn from a sight to make your eyes sore into somebody passable, then there's hope for you, too. You just might turn from an ugly duckling into a swan one of these days like happened in a story I once read."

"I do wish it would hurry up and happen if it's ever going to," Slade declared wistfully. "I've been trying to get a foot in the door with a girl that's traveling on this train but so far no luck, none."

"What's her name, the girl? Maybe, should I meet her, I could put in a good word with her for you."

"Her name's Ada Murdoch."

Gabe almost flinched.

"She's pretty as a speckled pup under a red wagon, Ada is. She's got hair as soft as sunlight. She's got skin as smooth as silk."

"You've touched it, her skin?"

"Oh, no. No such luck. She'd never let me, though I've tried courting her. I didn't get anywhere with her. She told me she prefers older men."

Gabe tried to keep a straight face. Older men indeed, he thought.

"Well, I'll be moseying on, Mr. Conrad." With a wave, Slade turned his horse and headed toward the line of wagons on his right.

Not toward just any wagon, Gabe noticed. Toward the Murdoch wagon which was being driven by Jack Murdoch with a sullen Ada sitting silently slumped, at his side only her eyes alert.

Gabe, without being too obvious about it, watched as Slade pulled up beside the wagon and began riding next to it. He couldn't hear the words that were exchanged among the trio but he noted the stony looks Jack Murdoch gave the youngster.

Mudoch gestured peremptorily—a gnarled thumb jerked over his shoulder. Pouting, Ada climbed into the wagon. Murdoch's arm shot out, his index finger pointing at Slade and then to the front of the train. Slade, obviously crestfallen, dropped back and let the Murdoch wagon roll on without him.

The course of true love never runs smooth, Gabe thought. He spurred his horse sometime later when he saw, through a haze of dust, Ed Brock stand up in his stirrups and signal for a halt.

Within minutes, people were climbing down from their parked wagons and building cook fires as they set about making their nooning.

Gabe followed their example. He found a shady spot beneath a cottonwood that grew along the bank of a shallow stream. There he unpacked some of the provisions Purcell's mule had been carrying and made himself a meal of them along with some water from the creek. He had not finished his far from regal repast—dried apples and a few figs—when he saw Ed Brock standing some distance away. The man was rolling a quirly. Gabe rose and, chewing on a fig, made his way toward the wagon master.

But, by the time he reached the spot where Brock had been, the wagon master was gone. Gabe looked around. There was no sign of the man.

"Excuse me," he said to a woman who looked worn with toil as she used an iron poker to stir up her fire. "Did you happen to see which way Mr. Brock went?"

The woman barely glanced at Gabe as she pointed to a grove of trees growing some distance away.

Gabe touched the brim of his hat to her, thinking, Brock's no doubt gone to answer a call of nature, or I miss my guess. He decided to wait for the man to reappear.

Time passed. He watched the woman worrying her fire. He listened to the strains of music produced by an accordion and a Jew's harp in the hands of two elderly men seated on barrels not far away.

More time passed.

Brock didn't reappear.

But Jack Murdoch emerged from the grove and went his way, looking neither right nor left.

As the minutes dragged by, Gabe felt a sense of uneasiness begin to creep over him. Brock should have returned by now. What could he be doing over there in the woods all this time? He decided he would go and find out. He wanted to know what it was the wagon master had wanted to talk to him about in connection with Purcell's murder. So he headed for the woods.

He was halfway to the trees when a woman burst out of them with her hair and skirt flying, running in his direction. As she came closer to him, he could see the stricken expression on her face. Her lips were twisted in a grimace and her eyes looked wild. Even so, he noted, she was a good-looking lady. Her face was the face of an angel—smooth, soft, and lovely, framed by auburn hair which reached halfway down her back. At the moment, however, it was the face of an angel in pain.

"What's wrong?" he asked her as she practically ran into his arms.

"I—he—" She looked over her shoulder and pointed to the trees. "In there—I think he's dead."

"Who's dead?"

"Mr. Brock."

"In the woods over there?"

She nodded and wiped the tears that were beginning to flow from her lovely hazel eyes.

Gabe gripped her upper arms to stop her from trembling. "You stay here," he told her in a soft voice, meant to calm her. "I'll be right back."

He left her then and sprinted toward the trees. As he entered the grove moments later, he felt a welcome coolness from the shade. He moved slowly forward among the trees looking for Ed Brock. It took him several minutes to find the man, and when he did, he halted and stared down at the body of the wagon master which lay on its back at the base of a tree with arms flung out. Open eyes stared upward.

Gabe let out the breath he hadn't realized he had been holding and got down on one knee beside the body. He pressed two fingers against the side of the wagon master's neck. They told him what he already suspected. No pulse was present. Brock's heart had stopped.

Gabe looked around, not sure what he was looking for. Then he looked back at Brock. The man's face was bloodless, an alabaster mask.

Gabe rose and turned to find a small crowd of people, Ada and Jack Murdoch among them, along with the woman who had alerted Gabe to Brock's condition, making their uneasy way toward him.

"Is it true?" Ada piped shrilly. "Is Mr. Brock dead?"

"He's dead," Gabe said.

"He must have had another one," the woman who had discovered the body murmured, her voice unsteady.

"Another what?" Gabe asked her as she stood staring down at Brock, an expression of distaste on her pretty features.

"Another heart attack," she whispered, her voice soft. "He had one before. About a week ago. He passed out cold but came out of it after awhile."

Gabe glanced at the crowd.

"He was always getting chest pains," a man volunteered. "Pains in his left arm. In his jaw, too. He tried to make a joke out of it. 'My ticker's not keeping proper time,' he'd say, and then he'd laugh. Looks now though. like it weren't no laughing matter."

A woman in the crowd began to weep. Through the hands covering her face, Gabe heard her cry, "I'm so tired of buryin' people. I wish I'd never left Pennsylvania. I didn't know when I was well-off."

"What are we going to do now?" Ada asked no one in particular. "Now we ain't got nobody to guide us through the mountains, what with Mr. Brock done gone to glory."

No one answered her.

Gabe turned to Jack Murdoch. "You were in these woods a little bit ago. I saw you come out. Did you happen to see Ed Brock while you were here?"

"I didn't see nobody or nothin'," Murdoch muttered.

"Ma'am, your name is—" Gabe prompted, addressing the woman who had told him about finding Brock.

"Gwen Landon."

"Did you see—"

"You know I saw him. I told you so."

"Excuse me, I was about to ask you if you saw anything suspicious when you were here earlier."

"No, I didn't see a thing suspicious. Not, that is, until I almost fell over him." She pointed to Brock's corpse. And then added, "There's nothing suspicious about a heart attack."

"Do you mind my asking why you were in these woods?"

Gwen blushed.

Rather prettily, Gabe thought. "I see," he said. "You didn't see Mr. Murdoch when you were here about your personal business?"

Gwen shook her head, not looking at Jack Murdoch who was glaring at her.

"Did you see Miss Landon, Mr. Murdoch?" Gabe inquired.

"I told you once I didn't see nothin' or nobody." Murdoch cleared his throat, a rumbling sound. "We'd best see to the burying. Some of the ladies, they'll sew a shroud to wrap the body in. We got no wood for a coffin, so we'll just have to put him in the ground pretty much the way he is."

Several of the women turned and left the woods. Gabe looked down at Brock's body as several of the men, Murdoch among them, moved forward to do their sad duty.

"Wait a minute," he said, as Murdoch and his companions bent down to pick up the body. He got down on one knee beside the corpse and then looked up at the men, who were watching him intently.

"Look," he said, pointing to the corpse. "You see what I see?"

The men looked at the body, then looked at Gabe. They exchanged puzzled glances.

Murdoch barked, "What's there to see but a dead body from which the immortal soul has fled?"

"His coat's buttoned up wrong," Gabe pointed out. "It's buttoned on the right side instead of on the left."

No one said anything.

"His coat—it's double-breasted," Gabe said. "It's buttoned on the right. That's the way women button their coats. Men button them on the left."

Once again the men exchanged glances.

"So what?" one of them finally asked.

"Brock wouldn't button his coat that way."

Gabe bent down and unbuttoned Brock's coat to reveal a mass of bloody white muslin beneath it. He looked up at the men who were watching him.

"Brock didn't die of a heart attack," he said. "He was shot to death. Here's where the round went into him—right through this muslin. Somebody shot him, using the cloth to muffle the sound of the round and to soak up the blood. Then whoever it was buttoned up his coat—only they did it wrong. Whoever killed him figured we would all think he died of another heart attack so nobody would be likely to ask any questions. We'd just put him in the ground and cover him up, and nobody'd ever be the wiser as to what really happened to him. *I* wouldn't have been if I hadn't happened to notice the way his coat was buttoned the wrong way."

"Can we carry him away now?" Murdoch asked gruffly.

Gabe rose and gestured to indicate that the men could do as they wished.

They bent and picked up the corpse and carted it away. Gabe followed them, stopping in the last of the shade at the edge of the grove to watch the grim procession. Gwen Landon and Ada Murdoch passed him. He hardly noticed the two women as thoughts whirled in his mind. Other people also left the cover of the trees and followed the men bearing Brock's body.

Gabe's eyes fell on the figure of Jack Murdoch who was bent over the grisly burden. Murdoch had been in the woods. Gabe's eyes shifted to Gwen Landon. So had she. Had she shot Brock to death?

Where was the weapon? The gun that someone had used to shoot the wagon master? Gwen Landon hadn't been carrying one when she emerged from the trees and neither, as far as Gabe could tell, had Jack Murdoch. Unless Gwen had hidden the gun in the woods after doing the deadly deed. Maybe Murdoch was carrying a hide-out gun in his boot or in a shoulder holster. Had anyone else, other than Gwen and Murdoch, been in the woods at the same time as the wagon master? Gabe glanced to the left and then to the right. He gazed across the flatlands to the wagons and to the spot where he had made his nooning. It was possible, he realized, for someone to have come out of the woods on the north side and to have made his or her way back to the train without him having been able to see the person.

An interesting puzzle. Also, an infuriating one. Infuriating because he was sure that Brock had known something that he thought related to the murder of Oscar Purcell and the man had intended to reveal that something to him. But Brock, as it turned out, never got the chance to do so. Someone had killed him before he could say what was on his mind.

Was that the reason for the killing?

Gabe shook his head in chagrin. He just couldn't be sure, one way or the other. Who knew what situation or circumstance had led to the killing? It could be anything. A lover's quarrel. A matter of money. Love and money, he speculated. They were, more often than not, one or both of them together, at the bottom of crimes of all kinds, murder very much among them.

CHAPTER SIX

Gabe stood on a grassy knoll under a cloudy sky that was threatening rain and watched as a pair of men went about the sad drudgery of digging a grave to receive the mortal remains of Ed Brock. The thudding of the shovelfuls of earth they dislodged hitting the ground above their bent backs made a sorrowful sound in the stillness.

The body of the wagon master lay on the ground beside the hole wrapped in a canvas shroud with lines of black stitches that looked like carpenter ants crisscrossing it. It was straight and smooth except for one end where the head formed a bulbous ball.

That's what we all come to, Gabe found himself thinking. Sooner or later. It's just a matter of time. The thought didn't depress him. Might as well be depressed over the fact that the sun would set each and every day, he reasoned. There was nothing much a man could do about it—not in the end, there wasn't. No use fretting about what a man can do nothing about.

The trick was to stave off the inevitable for as long as possible. One had to learn not to be foolhardy, not to take unnecessary chances which might leave one with a bullet hole somewhere in one's body or the blade of a knife between one's ribs. Let Death wait for what was due. Death was patient.

"Anybody want to say some holy words?" one of the grave diggers asked as he climbed, sweaty and smudged with dirt, out of the gaping hole in the ground.

No one answered him. People looked at one another or at the ground. No one moved.

"How about you, Amos Digby?" the other grave digger asked as he, too, climbed out of the hole, dropped his shovel, and wiped his dirty hands on his twill trousers. "You're a Bible-quoting man. I've heard you myself. Why don't you step on up here and give Ed Brock a proper sort of send-off?"

The man named Amos Digby had the face of a granite cliff and the fiery-eyed stare of an Old Testament prophet. "I ain't no anointed preacher," he declared in an oddly aggrieved tone.

"We're not, none of us, about to question your credentials, Amos," the grave digger stated. "Neither will the Lord God Almighty, I'll wager. So step on up here and say what needs to be said."

Amos Digby strode forward until he was standing at the edge of the grave. He looked down into it and then at the grave diggers. As if in response to an unspoken command of Digby's, they picked up two coils of rope and slid them beneath Brock's body.

Two other men silently joined them. With four men on the four ends of the two ropes, they swung the body out over the empty grave. In a moment, the grave was no longer empty.

They withdrew the ropes, which made a rustling sound as they slid under the canvas shroud, and stepped back as if they wanted to get well out of the way of something dark and unpleasant.

"Lord," Amos Digby intoned as he took a Bible from his pocket, "we're here to give You back one of Your own. Fellow name of Edward Brock. Not a saint, was he. Not much of a sinner either, though he did have him a quick temper and a taste for the red-eye. But You know all about that, so I won't go into it here and now.

"Open up Your pearly gates, Lord, and let old Ed amble on in to where the Glory's shining as bright as any sunrise and the eyes of all the angels assembled around Your heavenly throne are dazzled and delighted by it."

There was more, but Gabe paid little attention to the rest of Amos Digby's words. He was thinking about something Digby had said as he held his Bible above his head like a sword. He had said that Brock had had a temper. Gabe recalled the fact that Hal Slade had told him earlier in the day that Brock had had a fistfight with Jack Murdoch. Was the fact that the wagon master was noted for his temper the reason he had died? Had he angered someone enough to make that someone want to kill him?

"So he's gone and shuffled off this mortal coil, Lord," Amos Digby intoned, his eyes turned heavenward, "and now he's all Yours to do with as You see fit. Treat him kindly, Lord. He'd have done the same for You had he found You in the same kind of fix he's in at the moment."

Amos Digby slapped his Bible shut and stepped back. The people turned and began to leave the grave site. The pair of grave diggers picked up their shovels.

Gabe listened to the melancholy sound of clods of dirt striking the remains of what had once been a living man. He walked away, too. As he was passing Jack and Ada Murdoch, who were making their way back to their wagon, he heard Murdoch mutter, "Good riddance to bad rubbish, if you ask me."

He watched the pair as they made their way along with the rest of the mourners toward the wagons. Ada's over-the-shoulder seductive smile directed at Gabe was missed by her father who was walking several steps ahead of his daughter.

The people stopped when they reached the wagons, and an animated conversation promptly ensued among them. Gabe was too far away to hear what they were talking about, but he was keenly aware that many of them glanced in his direction as they talked. Then Hal Slade pointed at Gabe and said something to the others.

Jack Murdoch raised a fist and pounded it into the palm of his other hand, shaking his head vigorously as he did so. There was a great deal of gesticulating, and then voices rose in anger, allowing Gabe to make out a word here, a phrase there.

"No!" Murdoch bellowed.

"But we need—" from a woman with white hair which was drawn back from her lined face and gathered in a neat bun at the nape of her neck.

Intrigued, Gabe continued watching, knowing that whatever was going on had something to do with him.

After several more minutes passed, silence fell on the crowd. It was broken when the elderly woman said something. Two people promptly raised their hands. Then another one did the same. And another. Soon there were a score of hands raised. Only a few of the assembled people kept their hands at their sides, Jack Murdoch conspicuous among them. The woman spoke to Hal Slade, who promptly ran in Gabe's direction.

"Mr. Conrad," he said breathlessly when he reached Gabe and came to a halt. "We took a vote."

So that's what the hands were raised for, Gabe thought. He asked, "A vote about what?"

"You."

"Me?"

"Come on. The Widow Lane sent me to fetch you."

As Slade started back the way he had come, he glanced beseechingly over his shoulder.

Gabe shrugged and followed him over to the waiting crowd of people. When he reached them, the woman with the white hair stepped forward and said, "We haven't met, Mr. Conrad, but I've heard about you. Good things, I've heard. I understand you cured the Fergusons' sick cattle. I sent young Hal to bring you to us so we could tell you of our decision. By the way, my name is Audra Lane."

"Your decision, ma'am?" Gabe inquired.

"A majority of us has agreed to ask you to lead us the rest of the way to California now that our wagon master, Mr. Brock, has gone to meet his Maker."

The Widow Lane's statement took Gabe completely by surprise. But it didn't displease him. Far from it. If they wanted him to guide them, then he would do it, and in the doing of it he might succeed in uncovering the identity of the murderer of Oscar Purcell, not to mention Ed Brock.

"What do you say, Mr. Conrad?" an eager Slade prompted. "Will you do it?"

"We hope you will," the Widow Lane said, her eyes on Gabe's face.

"Not all of us hope you will," a male voice said sharply.

Gabe turned and saw that it was George Gordon who had just spoken.

"We all know you're here because you think someone among us murdered a friend of yours," Gordon added.

"That spells trouble for us," barked a man Gabe did not know. "You're just here to stir up a hornet's nest for good, God-fearing folk."

"I'm not here to stir up trouble for anybody except whoever it was killed my friend," Gabe responded evenly.

The man who had just spoken grunted his disbelief.

" 'The wicked flee when no man pursueth,' " Mrs. Lane quoted from the Bible, giving the nameless man a meaningful glance. " 'But the righteous are as bold as a lion.' "

"I say we try to make it west on our own," Gordon suggested. "We don't need him and his meddling." He nodded in Gabe's direction.

"I'm in favor of that," Gwen Landon put in firmly.

"What Mr. Conrad just said is true," Mrs. Lane argued. "He's not here to cause us trouble, not those of us who are innocent of any crime. And we need help, that's clear as well water. There's a steep grade facing us a few miles from here. Mr. Gordon was scouting the trail ahead, and he saw it."

"How's he going to help us get down it, that's what I want to know," a woman said. "What's he going to do that we can't do for our own selves?"

"That's enough, Janet," said a man standing beside the woman who had spoken. "Pay my missus no mind, Mr. Conrad," he continued. "She never did learn to bridle that tongue of hers."

"Gabe's still got my vote," Hal Slade announced, his eyes roving from face to face as if he were daring someone to try to argue with him.

"I'll tell the truth of the matter," Gabe said, "so there won't be any misunderstanding. You're right. I'm here to find a killer and bring him to justice. But I'm not here to make trouble for the innocent, like Mrs. Lane just pointed out. The fact of the matter is, I might be of some help to you—"

"You've already helped me and mine."

Gabe glanced to the left and saw that Henry Ferguson and his family had joined the group. "My oxen are fit as two new fiddles, thanks to you, Mr. Conrad."

"I think I can help you folks get down the mountain slope up ahead without you losing any of your wagons," Gabe said.

"You've had experience leading a wagon train?" Janet's husband asked.

"No," Gabe admitted. "But I've traveled with one or two in my time and learned a few tricks of the trail which might be of some help to you all."

"Sheep!" Gordon spat. "You're nothing but a bunch of silly sheep, the lot of you. No brains and no backbones is what you've all got." He turned and angrily walked away.

"Well, Mr. Conrad?" Mrs. Lane prompted. "Will you take on the responsibility of leading us to California?"

"I will," Gabe said without hesitation.

The following morning, Gabe turned Oscar Purcell's horse and pack mule over to the man who cared for the company's extra stock and then walked through the area enclosed by the wagons which were still locked together in a circle from the night before.

He greeted people as he passed them, introduced himself to men and women he had not met previously, offered a word of advice or encouragement, then moved on. The smell of food cooking tantalized his nostrils as he made his rounds. A badger was browning on a spit over a fire. A woman was rolling dough for friedcakes on a breadboard while fat sizzled in the spider, the three-legged skillet she had placed on the coals of her fire. More than one family invited him to share their breakfast, but he politely refused all such invitations, preferring to eat by himself and thus not show any favoritism among the emigrants in order to avoid unwanted hostilities arising out of petty jealousies.

But he did not refuse the soda bread Ada Murdoch brought him as he ate alone later by his own cook fire. "I thank you kindly for thinking of me," he told her as he accepted her offering. "This smells awful good."

"It tastes even better."

Gabe bit into the crusty bread and had to admit that Ada was right.

"I'll be seeing you," she said suddenly and made a beeline for the spot where Hal Slade was blowing on some kindling to start a fire for his own breakfast. Gabe watched her hunker down near Slade, her skirt raised and baring not only her ankles but her calves as well. Slade, Gabe noted, looked flustered as a result of her presence. Then she was up and racing back to the wagon she shared with her father. A moment later, she raced back to Slade carrying a small wicker basket brimming with soda bread. Gabe smiled to himself as he watched Slade fumble with and then drop the two-pronged fork he had been using to hold a piece of meat over the flames of his fire.

The boy's as nervous as a cat with six kits, he thought. But then, who can blame him? Having Ada around's enough to make most any man fidgety.

Less than an hour later, Gabe mounted his gelding and gave the order to hit the trail. The wagons were unlocked, the oxen were yoked and moved out. The wagons struggled along in a ragged line that gradually straightened itself out as they began the day's journey which would, if the weather held, see them cover fifteen or so miles before the sun went down.

Gabe found himself riding beside the wagon being driven by the Widow Lane. He gave her a good morning and touched the brim of his hat to her.

"I'm truly relieved to have you guiding us, Mr. Conrad," she told him as she deftly drove her pair of yoked oxen. "I was afraid you wouldn't want to take on the responsibility."

"I was honored to think you'd ask me—some of you, at any rate—to be your wagon master, ma'am. If there's anything I can do to help you at any time, why you just holler, and I'll come running. I heard all about your trouble."

Mrs. Lane sighed and shook her head. "You know then that I lost my man back along the trail."

"That's what I meant, yes."

"Arthur was a good man, Mr. Conrad, and a good provider. We thought we'd start a brand new life together out in California. Arthur had it in mind to start a vineyard and learn how to turn his harvests into wine. But it was not to be. The good Lord had other plans for my husband, and who am I to argue with them? But his loss still sits heavy on my heart, I must admit."

"I've no doubt of the truth of what you say, ma'am."

"When Arthur died, I wanted to give up. I was on the verge of turning around and going back home. But then I asked myself, what would I do there? Don't be a fool, Audra, I told myself. There's nothing for you back there now. And you might get lost if you try to head back there alone. Besides which I reckoned that Arthur would think me a quitter if I did that. So I didn't do it. I'm going to grow grapes, Mr. Conrad, when I get to where I'm going. That's what Arthur would have wanted me to do. I'll be doing it for him as well as for myself. I'll make him proud of me. That's what I vowed the day I almost gave up and turned back."

"You're a woman of spirit, Mrs. Lane."

She gave a little laugh and looked at Gabe, amusement dancing in her brown eyes. "I'll tell you a secret, Mr. Conrad. It was not spirit that kept me going. It was just plain old stubbornness or, as my father would have put it, bullheadedness. He always did say I was stubborn as any mule yet born."

Gabe gave her a smile and a wave and moved on, spurring his gray until he was at the head of the train. Later that morning he held up a hand to call a halt. They had reached the steep drop that Mrs. Lane had mentioned. He sat his saddle, staring at it. The ground dropped down at a forty-five-degree angle from the crest of the tableland where they had halted. The trail down was smooth, which indicated that other wagons had traveled it in the past. As did the broken remains of several wagons which littered both sides of the steep trail.

"How in the world are we ever going to get down there?" asked a woman who had stepped down from her wagon and come up alongside Gabe.

"We'll make it, Mrs. Gordon," he replied, recognizing the woman as George Gordon's wife, Martha, with whom he had chatted briefly earlier in the morning.

"George says we ought to detour so we can avoid attempting such a dangerous descent."

"We could do that," Gabe said. "But we'd have to go a good many miles out of the way to do it, and I don't think that's such a good idea. From what folk have told me, they're running low on provisions, and the longer we're on the trail, the worse that situation's going to get. I don't want to see people going hungry."

"So you're bound and determined to make it down to the valley below come hell or high water," George Gordon commented as he appeared to stand beside his wife.

Gabe suppressed the annoyance the man's remark had aroused in him. "I am, and so let's be about the business of getting down there."

Before Gordon could say anything more, Gabe dismounted and called out an order for the men to bring chains and ropes. He had no sooner done so than Martha Gordon, who was walking back to her wagon with her husband, faltered and began to tremble.

He went to her and asked, "What's wrong?"

"Nothing," she said, shaking her head.

Gabe noticed the sheen of sweat on her face.

"Martha's been feeling poorly the last day or so," Gordon explained. "She'll be alright once her nausea passes."

"Thank you for your kind concern, Mr. Conrad," Martha Gordon said in a voice that sounded disturbingly weak to Gabe. She took her husband's offered arm and they walked on.

"What do we have to do to get down there safely, Mr. Conrad?" one of the men Gabe had met earlier asked.

"First off, we chain the wheels of all the wagons. I want them double-locked so they can't spin so much as a fraction of an inch. Now, if you gents'll gather around, I'll show you how to go about doing that."

Gabe took a length of chain from the hands of one of the men and knelt down on the ground beside one of the wagons. "Pay close attention, gents," he directed as he wrapped the chain first around the right front wheel and then the left. "Do like this," he ordered. He linked the chain through the two rear wheels and then fastened it to the wagon box.

"I don't get it," Hal Slade said, taking off his hat and scratching his head. "If the wheels won't budge—I mean, the wagons won't roll down the hill, will they?"

"Nope," Gabe said, straightening up. "The wagons sure enough won't roll, and that is the whole point."

Slade and the rest of the men stared at Gabe with puzzled frowns on their faces.

"Hand me one of those ropes," Gabe said, holding out his hand. When one of the men gave him a length of rope, he proceeded to tie it around the bed of the wagon. He tested it when he had it in place and then loosened the knot he had made and drew it even tighter. When he was satisfied with what he had done, he explained, "Now what we'll do is we'll all get a good hold on this rope and then skid the wagon down the slope nice and slow."

"But what about the oxen?" Henry Ferguson asked. "Won't they be liable to get hurt that way?"

Gabe was momentarily taken aback by the question. He thought the matter of the oxen was self-evident, but apparently it was not. At least not to Henry Ferguson.

"You unyoke your oxen, Ferguson," he said patiently. "Your wife can drive them down the slope. After you and she have lightened your load some."

"Lightened our load?" Ferguson asked.

Gabe nodded. "Most of these wagons are too heavily loaded for the straight and narrow, never mind about a hill as steep as the one facing us. So unload most of your belongings, Ferguson. Heavy items like furniture—that sort of thing. You can tote them to your wagon later when it's safely down in the valley."

"I'll lend the others a hand," Slade volunteered, "since, like you, Mr. Conrad, I don't have a wagon of my own to worry about."

"That's neighborly of you, son. You go and do that."

When Slade had gone whistling away, Gabe picked up his dangling reins and led his gray back to Mrs. Lane's wagon.

"I came to get your wagon ready to make the trip down into the valley," he told her. "I'd be obliged if you'd drive it up to the crest of that hill yonder. Get it as close to the edge as you safely can, which won't be easy since it's getting crowded up there."

"I'll do the best I can, Mr. Conrad."

He rode beside her as she maneuvered her wagon into place and then climbed down from it.

"What now?" she asked him.

"Unyoke your oxen and drive them off to the side." As Mrs. Lane proceeded to do as she had been told, Gabe climbed up on one of the wagon's front wheels and peered through the opening in the canvas cover. The wagon bed was piled high with provisions and household goods. He began to remove some of them, placing them on the ground beside the wagon.

Mrs. Lane looked up at him from where she stood with her oxen, but she made no comment.

Once he had her wagon's load lightened substantially, he used chains and rope he had found among her possessions to lock the wagon's wheels in place and bind them to the wagon bed. When he was finished, he went over to Mrs. Lane and told her why he had done what he had.

"It's a risky business we're facing, isn't it?" she asked him when he finished speaking.

"Yes, ma'am, it is. I won't deceive you on that score."

"Well, it's got to be done, that's all there is to it."

Gabe heard the resignation in her tone. Resignation and something else. A trace of fear.

"We'll lower your wagon once we've got most of the others safely down into the valley," he said. "The men'll have had some experience by that time with what they're doing so there'll be less chance of trouble with your wagon. After we get it down, I'll give you a hand toting your belongings down the hill to it."

"Mr. Conrad, I hope you don't mind me making a personal comment." When Gabe offered no objection, Mrs. Lane continued, "You remind me of my late lamented husband. Arthur was a lot like you. Always ready to lend a hand to somebody in need. It's a trait I admired in him, as you might imagine. It's one of the many reasons I loved him so."

Gabe smiled and took his leave of Mrs. Lane. He walked to the crest of the hill, leaving his gray hitched to the ground behind him.

"Who's first?" he called out.

Immediately, a man with braided brown hair raised his hand.

Gabe beckoned to the other men to join him at the rear of the volunteer's wagon. They did, each of them getting a grip on the length of the rope that was fastened to the wagon they were about to lower into the valley.

"Dig in your heels, gents," Gabe told them, bracing himself and getting a firm grip on the rope. "Alternate positions on either side of the rope so we'll all have room to maneuver."

He glanced over his shoulder at the men behind him and then turned to the men in front of him. "You boys up front there, give the wagon a push to get it started."

The men obeyed, putting their shoulders against the wagon's tailgate to ease it over the crest of the hill.

"Now hold on for dear life!" Gabe yelled as the rope went taut and the wagon began to skid down the hill, dragging the men with it.

But they dug in their heels as Gabe had told them to do and, grunting and straining, they managed to keep the wagon from getting away from them. Like them, Gabe pulled hard on the rope, praying it wouldn't get away from him and that he wouldn't be dragged down the hill behind the wagon as it tore loose from those who would restrain it.

The rope held. The men held. The wagon inched slowly down the slope. So did the men behind it. One of them stumbled and went down. But he never lost his grip on the rope and was back on his feet and again holding his own within seconds.

Up above the men, on the crest of the hill, people had gathered and were watching in a tense silence.

The wagon slid down—almost imperceptibly. The only sounds were the grunting and groaning of the men holding the rope that kept it from careening down the slope and dragging them with it.

None of them could see their goal so far below them. They could only hold on. The cords in Gabe's neck stood out. Blood drummed in his head. His heart strained against his ribs. Sweat streamed down his face.

An eternity seemed to pass. Then, suddenly, the wagon lurched, causing Gabe to momentarily lose his footing. Then the rope went limp in his hands.

The silence was shattered by loud cheering coming from the hill above the men who had safely lowered the first of the wagons to the valley. The men themselves joined the cheering, letting the rope drop from their hands which, in many cases, it had burned.

Gabe called out, "The owner of this wagon—come on down here and claim it."

Three people burst out of the crowd at the crest of the hill—the man with the braided hair, a woman, and a girl of about ten. All three of them slid almost merrily down the slope, smiles on their faces as dust flew up around them. Then they were all shaking the hands of the men who had lowered their wagon, Gabe among them, and thanking them profusely for what they had just done.

"Get the rope and chains off that wagon," Gabe directed the man to whom it belonged, "and then push it over there out of the way. We've still got the rest of them to bring down here."

He beckoned to the other men, and they began to trudge together back up the slope. When they reached its crest, they walked over to a waiting wagon, put their shoulders behind it, and moved it up to the spot where it was to begin its perilous journey. They picked up the rope that had been tied to it, positioned themselves behind the wagon, and then, when Gabe gave a shout, they began lowering their burden.

By the time they had gotten the second wagon safely down into the valley, they were all soaked with sweat.

"This is getting to be like a treadmill," one of the men quipped as they climbed back up the hill.

The Ferguson wagon was the next to go down.

"Take care, boys," Ferguson cautioned as he and the other men picked up the rope he had tied to his wagon bed and began to push the wagon over the edge of the slope.

No one spoke as they leaned backward, their feet braced, and the wagon began its precarious descent toward the valley below.

The wagon tilted downward and began to skid, dust rising around it, its wheels digging into the ground. It hit a rut and tilted dangerously to the left, causing Gabe to order the men with him to shift to the right and pull on the rope as hard as they could to keep the wagon from overturning. Their mutual effort was at last successful.

Henry Ferguson sighed with relief.

Steadying the wagon but holding it motionless in place for a moment, the men gradually moved forward, easing the wagon down the sharp incline. Inch by inch, it slowly descended toward the verdant valley below.

The man behind Gabe cursed.

"What's wrong?" Gabe asked him without turning around.

"The damn rope burned my hand. I lost my grip on it for a minute, and the bloody thing slid through my hands and burned the hell out of them."

"Don't let it happen again," Gabe muttered through clenched teeth as he strained to maintain his hold on the rope.

"What do you think, I did it on purpose, for Christ's sweet sake?" the man asked angrily.

"Save your breath for the task at hand," Gabe shot back.

As they continued their strenuous efforts, the wagon continued to ease downward. Gabe was beginning to breathe a bit more easily when he thought he felt something: a change in the rope and in the rhythm the men were maintaining during the descent. His fingers tightened on the rope, turning white with the effort he was making.

"What the hell?" one of the men said. "What's going on?"

Gabe suddenly knew what was going on. Knew too what he had just felt—that subtle change he had sensed in the condition of the rope. It had slipped. Which meant—might mean—that it was coming unraveled.

He tensed, but the rope remained intact. So everything was alright, wasn't it? He wasn't sure, he had to admit. It seemed to him that there was more distance now between the first of the men working on the rope and the wagon itself than there had been moments earlier. Or was he imagining things?

No, he wasn't!

The knots that held the rope in place around the bed of the Fergusons' wagon were giving way. As Gabe stared at the back of the wagon, he could see them slipping. A sense of utter helplessness swept over him. There was nothing he could do to prevent what was about to happen. Nothing anyone could do.

"Oh my God!" someone cried in alarm.

It took Gabe a few seconds to realize that the cry had come from the throat of Henry Ferguson.

Then everything happened at once. The final knot gave way. The rope flew through the air toward the men pulling on it. It slashed the air above their heads before falling limply down on top of them. The wagon seemed to remain poised where it was for a moment. Then it began to move forward. Though its wheels didn't turn, it moved. Slowly at first and then faster.

Several of the men who had fallen to the ground when the rope gave way leaped to their feet and stared at it as if they were seeing something they couldn't—or wouldn't—believe. The wagon scraped harshly along the ground, its axles screaming. The canvas cover billowed on its curved bows.

"Stop it!" Ferguson screamed at the top of his voice.

But no one could stop the wagon now. It moved faster as it gained momentum. Within a matter of mere minutes it was rushing down the slope. Rocking crazily from side to side as it struck rocks and sank briefly into ruts, it nevertheless remained almost miraculously upright. But then, halfway down the slope, it seemed to come to a sudden halt for just an instant.

Gabe and the others could only watch in horrified silence as the rear of the wagon rose up into the air as if lifted by an unseen but giant hand and then looped forward to hit the ground. The goods remaining in the wagon flew out of both ends of it and through the air in the wake of the wagon which was tumbling end over end down into the valley.

It smashed to smithereens before finally coming to rest, what little was left of it, on the valley floor. Bows and boards and bent wheels careened through the air. Broken barrels of sugar and flour spilled their contents in two separate rains.

Moments later, it was all over. The crackling sounds the wagon had made as it disintegrated ended. The air was clear of debris.

Gabe became aware of a new sound. At first, he didn't recognize it for what it was. But then he did. He hung his head as his earlier sense of helplessness gave way to a feeling of profound sorrow for what had just happened.

Not far from where Gabe stood with his hands hanging at his sides, one of them still trailing the limp rope, stood Henry Ferguson with his shoulders hunched and his trembling hands hiding his face as he sobbed and his entire body shuddered as if it were suffering the onslaught of a wild unstoppable wind.

CHAPTER SEVEN

Gabe reached out and placed a hand on Ferguson's shoulder. "Get a grip on yourself," he said. "It's not the end of the world."

"It just as well might be," Ferguson sobbed, looking up at Gabe. "What will we do now, me and my family? How are we going to get to California with no wagon?"

"You'll make do. You've got your oxen. Your boys can ride on them. Somebody will give you and your wife a ride, no doubt."

"I don't want charity."

"You'll take it, Ferguson, or you'll walk."

"It's all my fault!" Ferguson wailed.

"What is?" Gabe asked sharply.

"That," Ferguson answered, pointing at the shattered remains of his wagon. "If I'd tied the rope—the knots—right, this wouldn't have happened. I'm not cut out for life on the trail. I let my oxen become poisoned. Before that, I broke an axle trying to take a shortcut. I didn't buy enough stores to last us throughout the trip. My wife has had to borrow from others to keep our bodies and souls together. I should never have set out on this trip. I should have stayed where I belonged, back where life is civilized. I'm not a rough-and-ready kind of man like you evidently are, Mr. Conrad. Back East in New Jersey, I was a newspaper reporter. I don't know the first thing about tying knots or caring for oxen or any of that kind of thing. I'm good for nothing out here. I can't do anything right!"

One of the men made a motion to stop Ferguson as he turned and began to trudge back up the hill, but Gabe prevented him from doing so.

"Let him go," he told the man. "Let him settle down some and get a hold on himself. He'll be alright."

"You're sure about that, are you?" The man asked. "I'm not so sure. He's all broke up."

"Let's get back to business," Gabe said. "We've got more wagons to bring down here. Are you still with me, gents?"

There were nods and murmurs of assent from the men who then followed Gabe back up the hill to where the rest of the wagons waited.

I should have checked Ferguson's knots and chains, Gabe told himself as he climbed, feeling guilty for not having done so. Like Ferguson said, he's no man of the trail. What happened is almost as much my fault as it is his.

When the men reached the crest of the hill, Gabe asked them to wait while he went from wagon to wagon checking the chains on each wagon's wheels and the way the ropes were fastened around the wagon beds. When he had finished the task, he rejoined the other men, and together they began to slide another wagon slowly down the steep slope to the valley below. The descent was without incident.

That evening, as Gabe was hunkered down and roasting the carcass of a rabbit he had shot when the traveling was done for the day, he looked up to find Mrs. Ferguson standing not far away and watching him. When she saw that he had noticed her, she came toward him and stopped on the far side of his fire.

"I hope you don't think I'm intruding on your privacy, Mr. Conrad. I thought I should come and speak to you."

"You're welcome at my fire, Mrs. Ferguson. What can I do for you?"

"Nothing. Well, there is something. I don't want you to feel that what happened this morning was your fault in any way."

"You're talking about the accident?"

"Yes, the accident. Henry knows it was his fault for not having properly knotted the rope. But I was afraid you would think we blamed you for not detouring as Mr. Gordon had suggested we do instead of trying to lower the wagons the way you chose to do."

"It seemed the best way to go for the reasons I gave you all at the time."

"I know."

"I told your husband what happened didn't mean you all were completely out of luck. You can ride with other families."

"A family named Pike has taken us under their wing. They're very nice people. But our possessions—we had to leave most of them behind. That was difficult to do. Of course, we did manage to salvage a few things. Small things. Keepsakes mostly. There simply wasn't room in the Pike's wagon, or in any of the others either for that matter, for our furniture and other things."

"I've been planning to talk to the other emigrants about their loads," Gabe said. "Most of the wagons, from what I've seen, are overloaded. Add to that the fact that the oxen and mules pulling those wagons aren't in the best of shape at this stage of the game and lightening the loads seems to me to be a thing that's got to be done, though I don't reckon my ordering it is going to make me many friends."

"I'll be going, Mr. Conrad."

"You stick by your man, Mrs. Ferguson. He's shaken up, as you know. He'll need a shoulder to lean on for a while."

"Henry's a good man, Mr. Conrad. When we get to California, he'll get a job with a newspaper out there, and then he'll do what he can do well, which is write."

"I myself," Gabe said, "can't seem to put two words together without I have to struggle with both of them. Some men are good at one thing and some at another. You make sure your husband understands that, won't you?"

Mrs. Ferguson's answer was an enthusiastic nod.

As she turned to leave, Gabe said, "Before you go, Mrs. Ferguson, I wonder, would you mind if I asked you a question or two?"

She turned back to him.

"I noticed that Jack Murdoch didn't seem all that upset by the murder of Ed Brock. Would you know what might account for that?"

"There was some bad blood between Mr. Brock and Mr. Murdoch."

"How come, do you know?"

"Mr. Murdoch accused Mr. Brock of—of raping his daughter, Ada."

Gabe whistled through his teeth. "That's a pretty serious charge. Did Mr. Murdoch have any proof concerning what he claimed happened?"

"I don't believe so. But then I really don't know the whole story of the incident, just what little I've heard about it."

"So Murdoch just more or less *suspected* Brock of—attacking Ada?"

"So I understand, but I may be wrong. Mr. Conrad, I really don't like to gossip so, if you don't mind, I'll be on my way."

"I understand how you feel, ma'am, but this is important. We're talking here about a murder."

"I thought you were concerned about finding out who murdered your friend—or so I've been told."

"I am. But I think there just might be a connection between that murder and the killing of your former wagon master. In fact, I think it's possible—maybe even likely—that the same person might have done in both men."

"Do you have any proof of that?"

"No, none. Just my suspicions." Gabe paused a moment and then asked, "Where were you when the murder of Mr. Brock took place, do you recollect?"

"I was washing clothes."

"Could you see the woods where the murder took place from where you were washing?"

"Yes, but what—"

"Did you by any chance see anybody enter or leave the woods before or after the murder?"

"Yes, I saw Mr. Murdoch—" Mrs. Ferguson halted in mid-sentence. "I think I see what you're getting at. You think Mr. Murdoch might have killed Mr. Brock."

"He might have, yes. He had a motive, according to what you've told me. Did you see anybody else go in or out of those woods around the time we're talking about?"

"No."

"When I was on my way to them, I ran into Gwen Landon. She'd been in the woods. In fact, she was the one who stumbled on Brock's body."

"I don't know anything about that. I didn't see Miss Landon enter or leave the woods."

"Where was your husband at the time Brock was gunned down?"

"Mr. Conrad, *really!*"

"I don't mean to make you mad, ma'am. I hope you'll try to understand that I have to ask questions like this if I'm ever to find out who—"

"My husband was with me. He was hanging the wash on our clothesline." Mrs. Ferguson seemed suddenly disconcerted. "I know most men don't do that sort of thing, but Henry has always helped out with domestic duties. I think that's an admirable trait. One more men would do well to emulate, in my humble opinion."

"I'm obliged to you, Mrs. Ferguson, for taking the time to answer what I know are troublesome questions."

"Good night Mr. Conrad."

So, Gabe thought as Mrs. Ferguson walked away, her shoulders squared and her spine stiff, Jack Murdoch had it in for Ed Brock. He considered that fact, turning it over in his mind. He came to the conclusion that it helped less than he might have liked. Jack Murdoch certainly had no motive for killing Oscar Purcell, though he did have one for doing in the wagon master. No, he corrected himself, that's not altogether true. Gold's a good enough motive to kill for. At least, it is for some folks. And if Murdoch killed Brock, it means he's not squeamish about shooting a man down in cold blood.

Gabe turned his attention to his meal which was sizzling on the spit. He turned the rabbit's carcass to brown it evenly and then, when the meat was done, removed it from the fire. After letting it cool a bit, he began to eat. When he was finished feasting on his kill, he stamped out his fire and, hitching up his jeans, made his way to the Gordon wagon.

He halted before he reached it when he saw Martha and George Gordon seated in rockers on the ground outside as twilight descended on the encampment. Gabe wanted to talk to Martha Gordon, but not in the presence of her husband. He retraced his steps, turned, and headed for the wagon that belonged to Gwen Landon.

He halloeed it when he reached it and was rewarded with Gwen's head popping through the opening in the canvas cover.

"Oh, it's you," she said, clearly disappointed.

He thought he read her correctly and decided to take a chance. "Were you expecting George Gordon?"

Her face paled. She looked around her as if to see if Gabe's question had been overheard by anyone. Then her face gradually grew crimson. Anger flared in her eyes.

"Just what the hell do you mean by that smart-aleck remark, Mr. Conrad?"

"I meant you seemed disappointed to see it was me called out. I thought you might not have been disappointed if it had been George Gordon who had done it. Am I right or am I wrong?"

"Mind your own business, Mr. Conrad."

When Gwen disappeared inside the wagon, Gabe stepped up on a front wheel and seated himself in the wagon seat. Pulling aside the wagon cover, he said, "I am minding my own business, Miss Landon. Which happens to be murder, as I made known to you and the rest of the folks traveling on this train."

"You don't think I had anything to do with the murder of Ed Brock, do you?"

"Did you?"

"I most certainly did not!"

"How about the murder of my friend Oscar Purcell?"

"Get out of here, Mr. Conrad. I've got nothing to say to you."

"So you won't talk. That makes me mighty suspicious, I have to tell you, Miss Landon."

"You and your suspicions be damned, Mr. Conrad."

"Have you forgotten the fact that I saw you come out of the woods the day Ed Brock was murdered in them?"

"So what?"

"You could have killed him and then put on an act like you'd just found the body and were as innocent as a newborn babe."

Gwen's lips twisted in a feral snarl. "Any why, pray tell, would I do that? I had no reason to kill Ed Brock."

"Didn't you?"

Gwen's snarl became a cry of utter outrage. "How *dare* you!"

Unfazed by her reaction, Gabe said, "The day I joined the train, I told Ed Brock about the murder of my friend, Purcell. He told me he had something to discuss with me about that but he didn't have time to do it right then and there. He said him and me could talk later. Well, as it turned out, we never did get to talk on account of somebody killed him and put an end to his talking once and for all.

"As a matter of fact, I happened to be on my way to talk to him in the woods where I'd seen him go when you came running out with the news that he was dead."

"He was dead when I found him. Let's get that straight, once and for all, Mr. Conrad. And as long as we're on the subject, I wasn't the only one in the woods the time you're talking about. Jack Murdoch was in there, too. Or have you forgotten that?"

"No, I've not forgotten that, Miss Landon. Are you by any chance suggesting that it was Murdoch who killed Brock?"

"I'm not suggesting anything. I'm just pointing out facts."

"Did you happen to see anybody else besides Murdoch in the woods when you were in them that day?"

Gwen's face relaxed into a smile. She began to laugh.

"What's so funny, Miss Landon?"

"You are, Mr. Conrad. You're funny. I wonder if the men who work at detecting crime for Mr. Allan Pinkerton are also funny men. I rather doubt it. Crime detection needs men of more serious mien."

"I'll try to be more serious about my crime detecting in the future."

"You're not very good at it, you know."

"I'm not? Maybe you could tell me where I've gone wrong."

"Well, for one thing, there was somebody else in the woods besides me and Mr. Murdoch around the time Mr. Brock was killed."

"Who was it?"

"You mean to say you don't know?"

"I didn't see anyone come out of the woods except you and Murdoch."

"That youngster, Hal Slade—he was in the woods. He said he was out hunting. Maybe he was out hunting Ed Brock."

"Why would he want to do that?"

"Why don't you ask him, Mr. Conrad?"

"You know something? I think I'll do that very thing." Gabe climbed down from the wagon.

As he walked away, he found himself regretting not having asked Gwen Landon about her relationship with George Gordon. He returned to her wagon.

"Miss Landon?"

Her head popped through the opening in the canvas. "Oh, it's you again."

"I hear you're friendly with George Gordon, Is that the truth?"

Gwen surprised Gabe by nodding her head and replying, "Of course it's true." She gave a mirthless laugh and added, "I'm friendly with everyone on the train."

"I saw Gordon coming out of your wagon the morning I arrived in your camp. It was just before the sun rose. Do you mind telling me what he was doing in your wagon instead of his own at that early hour?"

"I don't mind at all, Mr. Conrad. George had been out scouting and standing guard during the night. Ed Brock had the men stand guard on a regular schedule during the nights to make sure the people on the train would be safe. George had the last shift of the night you're referring to. When he returned to camp, he stopped by my wagon to borrow some coffee beans. It seems his wife had run out of them."

"Be seeing you, Miss Landon." As Gabe walked away, he thought back to the morning in question. He couldn't recall having seen Gordon carrying anything that morning. Of course, he realized, Gordon could have stuffed a sack of coffee beans into his pocket so that they wouldn't have been seen.

He made his way among the emigrants who were cooking supper as the twilight deepened into darkness. When he reached his destination—the Gordon wagon—he halted. Neither George nor Martha Gordon was in sight. The rockers they had been sitting in earlier were gone. He hesitated. He wanted to talk to them separately if possible. But he didn't know if they were both in the wagon. He could go instead and talk to Hal Slade, try to find out what Gwen Landon had meant about the possibility that Slade had been hunting Ed Brock the day the wagon master was murdered. Or he could go and talk to Jack Murdoch about the fact that the man had been nursing a grudge against Brock because of what he had supposedly done to Ada.

But he was here now. So he'd see how the land lay. If things didn't suit him, he'd move on to one of the other people he intended to talk to. He stepped up to the wagon's tailgate and rapped sharply on it as he would have knocked on the door of a house.

"Who is it?" a woman's voice called.

"Mrs. Gordon," Gabe said, "I stopped by to see how you're feeling."

Gabe's remark was met by silence. The silence was followed by the sound of movement inside the wagon. A moment later, the wagon cover was unlaced and Martha Gordon peered out at Gabe, the flames of a nearby cook fire lighting her features.

"I'm fine, Mr. Conrad, thank you."

She didn't look fine to Gabe. She looked sick. There was a sheen of perspiration on her face and a hectic flush on both of her cheeks.

"I'd invite you in," she said, "but my husband's not here, Mr. Conrad."

So she's a discreet woman and wife, Gabe thought.

"That's alright," he said. "I was on my way to talk to Jack Murdoch but thought I'd stop by and ask after you. I wonder, Mrs. Gordon, if you'd mind answering a few questions for me?"

Gabe saw her eyes flicker like those of a startled animal. "It won't take long," he promised.

"What do you want to know?"

Gabe reminded her of the morning he had joined the wagon train.

"I remember that day, yes," she responded warily.

"I was wondering, was your husband with you that night?"

"Was my husband—" Martha frowned. "Why, of course George was with me that night, as he is every night."

"*All* night?"

"Yes, all night. Why—"

"Mrs. Gordon, I've been told your husband was standing guard that night. He'd been out scouting, I was told, under orders from Ed Brock. So he couldn't have been with you all night, not if what I was told was true."

Martha's wariness turned to confusion. She blinked rapidly several times and ran the fingers of one hand through her disheveled hair.

"I—I remember now," she said at last. "You're quite right, Mr. Conrad. George was on guard and scout duty that night. I'd forgotten. One day or night on the trail is much the same as any other, is it not? But," she hastened to add, her words rushed and seeming to tumble over one another in her evident haste to utter them, "George was with me all the *rest* of that night."

"You're sure about that?"

"Certainly, I'm sure," Martha snapped, her eyes angry now. "Why are you asking me these questions?"

"Well, as you may recall, I'm trying to find out who killed my friend, Oscar Purcell. Not to mention Ed Brock."

"George is not a violent man, Mr. Conrad. Nothing could make him commit murder. I am sure of that."

"You said yourself, Mrs. Gordon, that one day on the trail's a whole lot like any other, so how you can be sure that your husband was with you on the day Ed Brock was killed?"

"I remember because—this is really most embarrassing, Mr. Conrad."

Gabe raised a questioning eyebrow.

"We were—George and I were engaged in—we were engaged in an intimate encounter at the time. That is why I remember where George was."

"Mrs. Gordon, I kind of hate to say this, but I feel I've got to if I'm to get to the bottom of these two killings."

Martha Gordon's wariness, Gabe noted, was back. It flared in her eyes and made all ten of her fingers drum on the wagon's tailgate as she waited to hear what he was going to say next.

"The morning I arrived in your camp for the first time, I saw your husband leaving Gwen Landon's wagon and entering his own—this one—a few minutes later."

Martha turned her head. The firelight shimmered in her hair, but her features were in darkness now.

Gabe shifted his position in order to see her face.

"George told me he stopped by Miss Landon's wagon after returning to camp that morning."

"Why did he do that? Do you know?"

"He—he told me he had heard her calling out from inside the wagon. He was worried that something might be wrong. It turned out that Miss Landon had simply been having a nightmare, he told me."

Somebody's lying, Gabe thought. The question was who. Gwen Landon? Or Martha Gordon?

Martha suddenly paled and swayed to one side.

"You alright, ma'am?" a concerned Gabe quickly inquired.

"I've been feeling sick to my stomach several times recently. So if you have no more questions, Mr. Conrad, I think I had better lie down and rest for a while."

Gabe did have a few more questions he wanted to ask her, but he decided now was not the time to ask them. "You take good care of yourself, ma'am. Do you want me to go hunt up your husband and send him home to you?"

"No!"

The word was spoken too loudly.

"No, Mr. Conrad," Martha repeated more softly. "That won't be necessary. Thank you anyway. I shall manage quite nicely by myself, I'm sure."

"I'll bid you good night then, ma'am."

Gabe walked away. He had not gone far when he saw in the distance the shadowy figure of George Gordon emerging from Gwen Landon's wagon. Old George, he thought, is as brazen about his adulterous affair as Gwen is bold about it. He found himself commiserating with Martha Gordon and wondering if she did or didn't know of her husband's betrayal of his marriage vows.

"Hello there," Ada Murdoch greeted him when he reached her wagon. "You've come to call on me, have you?"

"Not exactly, Ada," he replied. "I wanted to have a talk with your daddy."

Ada pouted. "I can't rightly reckon why you'd want to do that when here I am all hale and hearty and awful glad to see you again."

Gabe smiled. He tried to pay no attention to the lust that had begun to seethe within him as he gazed at Ada's ripe body which had been, and apparently still was, so willing and very able to give him the kind of pleasure that could send him soaring to the skies. He was, he discovered, not all that disappointed when Ada informed him that her father was not around.

"Where is he?"

Ada shrugged. "Playing poker with a bunch of his cronies."

"Where would that be exactly?"

"Over to old man Soames's wagon. Him and old man Soames, they're *addicted* to poker like some folks are to opium."

"Well, maybe I'll mosey on over to old man Soames's wagon and see if he's still there."

"Do you have to go right away? I mean right this very minute?"

Did he? Gabe knew very well that he didn't. But he had a responsibility to pursue the matter of the murders. Didn't that take precedence over what Ada seemed to have in mind?

Before he could come up with an answer to his question, Ada was standing against him, her pelvis rocking, her arms encircling his neck, her tongue licking her full lips.

"Don't go," she whispered. "We could do it again. In the wagon this time. You can talk to my pa any old time."

True enough, Gabe thought. Or just about. His arms went around Ada's warm and welcoming body. He bent his head and kissed her. First on the forehead. Then squarely on the lips.

A disturbing thought pushed its way into his mind. "Your daddy—when's he due back here?"

"I don't know for certain. But he sometimes spends the whole night playing poker. Doesn't get back till the crack of dawn. Why?"

"He might catch us at it."

"So don't take your clothes all the way off. That way, if he comes back unexpected, you can scamper quick like a mink out of the wagon before he finds out you're here.

I'll pretend to be sleeping. I'll snore. Like this."

Ada snored noisily.

Gabe had his misgivings, but they were overcome by the desire that was coursing through him, making his blood boil and his head spin.

"Come on," Ada said, practically dragging him inside the wagon with her.

He let himself be dragged, happy as a lark at the prospect of what lay directly ahead for him.

CHAPTER EIGHT

"Whoooeee!" Ada exclaimed, stretching luxuriously. "Now weren't that wonderful though?"

"Honey, it was ten times wonderful," Gabe enthusiastically agreed from where he lay contentedly flopped down beside her on the bed.

Ada leaned over and chucked him under the chin. "You look like the cat that ate the canary."

"I feel like that cat, too. Completely satisfied." But, Gabe thought, it's time I got back to the business at hand.

"Ada, honey," he began, "did your daddy ever show any violent tendencies?"

Ada withdrew her hand. She frowned sulkily at Gabe. "You want to talk about my pa at a time like this? I do declare, there must be something wrong with you."

Gabe propped himself up on his elbows and kissed her on the tip of her nose.

She smiled sweetly, her sulkiness disappearing.

But it quickly returned when Gabe asked her, "Who do you think killed Ed Brock?"

"Just what is this all about?" she asked, instead of answering his question.

"Well, you know I'm trying to find out who shot

Brock and who killed my friend."

"Well, my pa didn't do it, if that's what you happen to be thinking. Why don't you stop beating about the bush and say straight-out what awful thoughts you've got on your evil mind concerning my closest of living kin? Why don't you do that, huh?"

"I'm not saying your daddy did it," Gabe hastened to point out. "But to tell you the truth, it looks like he's a first-class suspect in the matter."

"Why? What makes you say a terrible thing like that?"

"On account of he was in the woods at the time Brock was shot down dead and on account of he had a real bad grudge against Brock that he's been nursing."

"Grudge? What might you mean by that?"

"I think you know very well what I mean by that."

Ada turned her head, tossed her hair, was silent for a long tense minute. Then, "My pa does have him a temper, that's true enough. But he wouldn't kill anybody."

"Lots of men have killed in a grudge fight."

"Not my pa. You're barking up the wrong tree if that's what you're thinking. The wrong tree entirely."

"I've been told that your daddy thinks Ed Brock took you against your will. Is that the truth?"

"Never you mind what's the truth and what isn't. I think it's high time you were on your way."

Gabe sat up. Reluctantly he pulled up his pants. He buttoned his fly and buckled his belt, his longing eyes on Ada's back which she had turned to him.

"And here," she muttered, "I thought you came here 'cause you'd taken a shine to me. But no, you came here to poke and pry and prod to try to get my pa up on a scaffold so he can be hanged by his neck until he's dead as a doornail. That's nasty!"

"Honey," Gabe began, reaching out for Ada.

She pulled away from him and pulled her dress down.

"Honey," he tried again, "I did truly take a shine to you. There's no denying that."

He waited, but Ada didn't relent; she kept her back to him and remained silent.

"Try to see this thing from my angle, will you?" he pleaded. "I can't rest till I run to ground the man or men—or woman or women, as the case may turn out to be—who killed Brock and Purcell."

Ada suddenly turned to face Gabe, fury flaring in her wide-open eyes. "Oh ho!" she cried, shaking a finger in his face. " 'Woman or women,' " she quoted. "Now you're saying you think *I* let light through Mr. Brock. Maybe you think I also killed your friend on whom I have never laid so much as a single eye in all my entire life!"

"Now, Ada, don't go and get your dander up. I didn't say any such thing."

"But you're *thinking* it. That's just as bad!"

"I am *not* thinking it," Gabe protested. But then an idea occurred to him which stopped him in his tracks. What if Ed Brock had indeed raped Ada? Wouldn't that constitute sufficient motive for murder on her part?

"Get out!" Ada ordered.

"Ada, if you'll just listen to me—"

"I've heard enough. Too damn much, as a matter of fact. Get out of here, Mr. Detective, and take your trouble-making elsewhere."

"Ada—"

"Git!"

Gabe got.

As he stepped out of the wagon and was about to climb down to the ground, he found himself face-to-face with none other than Ada's brawny father, Jack Murdoch, who stood with his beefy hands planted on his bulky hips as he stared up at Gabe.

"Good evening, Murdoch," Gabe greeted the man, somewhat sheepishly. "I was just inside having a talk with your daughter."

"What the hell have you and her got to talk about?" Murdoch barked.

"Well," Gabe drawled, stepping onto one of the wagon wheels and from there to the ground, "actually we were talking about who might have killed Ed Brock and Oscar Purcell."

"Ada knows nothing about that or them."

"So she indicated, so she indicated. But that doesn't apply to you, now does it, Murdoch?"

"What the hell are you getting at?"

"You were in the woods around the time Brock was shot to death. *That's* what I'm getting at. Did you do it?"

"What right have you got to ask me a question like that?"

"Did you do it?" Gabe pressed.

Ada's head appeared through the opening in the canvas cover. "He's just a busybody, Pa. Pay him no mind."

"Busybody, is he?" Murdoch muttered ominously, his attention shifting to his daughter. "What was his body busy about while he was in there alone with you just now?"

Ada glanced at Gabe and blushed. "He was paying a purely social call," she replied. "It was you he came to see, not me."

"But it seems he saw you."

Ada's blush deepened.

"Murdoch," Gabe said, "would you mind if I searched your wagon? I want to see if Purcell's gold turns up in your possession."

Like an enraged bull, Murdoch lowered his head and glared at Gabe. "I most certainly would mind. You keep your paws and prying eyes away from what's mine. That goes for my girl-child, too."

As a small crowd began to gather, sensing trouble, Gabe said, "I understand you had quite a grudge against Ed Brock for what you claim he did to your daughter."

Murdoch's eyes narrowed in his pale fleshy face, two black bullets in all that surrounding dough. "Claim? What do you mean by *claim*?"

"Were you there to see what supposedly happened between Brock and Ada?"

Murdoch sucked in a deep breath and let it out with a rush. "Damn you, Conrad, you'd better back off. You're about to step over the line. If you do, I'll beat you to within an inch of your lousy life. You hear me?"

"Maybe Ada tends to be free with her favors," Gabe said, wondering if he could unbalance Murdoch just enough to cause the man to make some statement in the heat of anger and distress which would be tantamount to a confession in the matter of Brock's murder.

Murdoch let out an enraged roar. His hands clenched at his sides. His lips worked wordlessly for a moment.

"You're as bad as Brock was," he finally managed to get out. "He came around like some rutting ram. Just like that young whippersnapper's been doing. That Hal Slade. If I catch him hanging around her again, I swear I'll slit his throat."

There were shocked gasps and exclamations from the crowd that had gathered.

"You sure do have yourself a hectic temper, Murdoch," Gabe observed. "Is it that temper of yours that led you to the killing of Ed Brock for what you say he did to your daughter?"

The sound that issued from Murdoch's mouth was neither a scream nor a bellow but a little bit of both. He lunged at Gabe and butted him with his lowered head. As Gabe was slammed backward to collide with the wagon wheel behind him, Murdoch punched him in the gut just below his ribs. He followed that punch with a right cross that connected with the left side of Gabe's head.

"Fight!" someone shouted gleefully. Men and women came running to join the onlookers.

Gabe dodged the next thrust Murdoch made, and the man let out an agonized howl as his fist slammed into the wagon wheel instead of Gabe. Murdoch did not let that stop him—or even slow him down. He stepped backward, pulling his hurt hand free of the wheel's spokes, and slammed it into his opponent's face, almost breaking Gabe's nose.

As blood began to flow from his nose, Gabe danced nimbly away from his attacker. Then, with both of his fists raised and his head lowered behind them, he sprang forward lightly on the balls of his feet and delivered a savage series of blows which struck Murdoch in the face, chest, and gut.

Murdoch grunted and staggered under the onslaught. Gabe took advantage of his unwilling retreat to move in on the man. He let fly with a left uppercut that caught Murdoch under the chin and snapped his head up to send his long hair flying.

Murdoch retaliated with a one-two punch that Gabe took without flinching. He followed that up with an attempt to knee Gabe in the groin. But Gabe managed to sidestep the attempt. Before Murdoch's leg could straighten out and his foot could return to the ground, Gabe seized the man's ankle and twisted it so hard that it forcibly turned Murdoch's entire body a full 180 degrees to the right.

Bellowing, Murdoch tried to seize Gabe but missed. Still bellowing, he went down, and dust flew up around him.

A few weak cheers went up from among the onlookers, but somebody—Gabe couldn't see who it was because of the thick haze of dust raised by Murdoch's fall—gave him a mocking catcall.

Murdoch, shaking hair and sweat out of his eyes, got shakily to his feet. With his fists thrust out in front of him, he lumbered forward and swung first his left fist, then his right. His left slammed like a sledge into Gabe's gut, bending him over. His right struck Gabe's lowered chin. Gabe's head was knocked backward, and blood sprayed from his battered nose.

Murdoch reached out and hit him again, harder this time, spinning Gabe around. He seized Gabe from behind, both of his huge arms encircling Gabe's body. He began to squeeze, lifting Gabe off the ground as he did so.

Someone in the crowd cheered as Gabe clawed desperately at Murdoch's hands which had fingers that seemed to be made of iron. He tried to break Murdoch's grip— but failed miserably to do so. He could feel the air being forced out of his lungs. He could feel, too, the sensation that was making a furnace of his chest. He knew what Murdoch was trying to do. Murdoch wanted to break his back. He let go of Murdoch's hands, and as he did so, Murdoch gave a grunt of satisfaction.

Gabe reached behind him. He seized Murdoch by the hair. He pulled Murdoch's head forward until it was touching his own neck and then, letting go with one hand and forming that hand into a rock-hard fist, he clubbed the top of Murdoch's head with it.

The maneuver worked. Murdoch's knees buckled. A moment later, he crumpled and fell to the ground, taking Gabe down with him. But he was far from finished. There was, Gabe soon discovered, a lot more fight left in him. Murdoch rolled over, dragging Gabe with him, until he was on top of Gabe. He straightened up, gripped Gabe's body between his knees, and squeezed. His hands snaked out and his thumbs landed squarely on Gabe's eyes. He began to try to gouge them out of Gabe's head.

Gabe fought hard to get out from under Murdoch. He twisted his head from side to side in a desperate attempt to prevent his opponent from blinding him. Finally, he managed to get a grip on Murdoch's left hand with both hands. He bent it backward and kept bending it.

Murdoch screamed.

Gabe chose that moment to bring both of his legs up. His knees slammed into Murdoch's body, sending the man flying over his head. He scrambled to his feet and stood over Murdoch, who was lying on his side in the dirt and staring up through bloodshot eyes at him.

Gabe blinked the sweat out of his eyes as he returned Murdoch's malevolent stare.

Ada appeared out of nowhere, an apparition in the billowing dust the two men had raised, and knelt beside her father. She stroked his cheeks and then kissed him, missing his lips, her own lips landing on her father's chin. She looked up at Gabe.

"Leave him alone, you bully!" she cried.

The irony of the situation almost made Gabe laugh. So he was the "bully" in Ada's eyes! So much for fairness when filial devotion clouded the picture.

"I'll gladly leave your daddy alone," he told Ada, "if he'll return the favor and leave me be."

"I'm going to kill you, Conrad," Murdoch snarled in a ragged voice. "You'd best watch your step from now on. I'll get you—and get even for the trouncing you gave me here today."

"You're going to kill me the way you killed Brock, you mean?" Gabe couldn't help remarking, knowing the words constituted something like a taunt.

"Damn you, I told you I never killed that son of a bitch!" Murdoch shouted, as he tried to struggle to his feet.

Ada managed to restrain him.

"I'm going to search your wagon, Murdoch," Gabe announced. "If you or anybody else makes a move to stop me, I'll blast you and them both clear from here to kingdom come."

Gabe waited a brief beat and then climbed into the Murdoch wagon. He searched through the belongings he found within it. After having gone through them in what he considered a thorough fashion and having found no trace of the gold that had belonged to Purcell, he returned to the scene of his fight with the wagon's owner.

Murdoch was up on his feet now, leaning on his daughter for support. His chest was heaving as he tried to catch his breath, and his eyes were alive with anger.

"I didn't find any gold hidden anywhere inside your wagon," Gabe told him. "But that doesn't necessarily mean that you didn't do in my friend. Nor does that fact have anything to do with letting you off the hook as a prime suspect in Brock's murder. I'll be keeping an eye on you, Murdoch."

"Conrad," Murdoch muttered, "you'd better, because, like I said, I'm going to kill you the first chance I get. You're a dead man, Conrad. I'm going to see that you go to your just reward before too much more time passes."

Gabe turned and walked away without looking back. He forced himself to remain calm in the face of Murdoch's violent threat, but he wanted to turn on his heels and go back and beat the man to a bloody pulp. He was still seething with rage when he felt a hand land on his shoulder. He raised his fist and spun around, expecting to see Murdoch. . . .

"What was that fracas all about?" a grinning Hal Slade asked him. "It looked to me like you and Mr. Murdoch were going at it fast and furious even before the howdys were over."

Gabe lowered his fist. He flexed his fingers, drew a deep breath, and let it out. "You might say we had a disagreement of sorts."

"He's hell on the hoof, that Mr. Murdoch is. You better watch your back from now on. I heard him say he means to kill you."

"You figure him for a back-shooter, do you?"

"No, not exactly. What I said, it was just a manner of speaking. What I meant was that you should steer clear of him from now on. Ever since I started trying to walk out of an evening with Ada, I've had to steer clear of her pa. He'd hide me with that bullwhip of his if he ever caught us sparking."

Gabe smiled and arched an eyebrow as he gazed at Slade. "So you've been sparking Ada Murdoch, have you?"

"Well, yes. Yes, I have. It's your fault."

"*My* fault?" an astonished Gabe exclaimed, jabbing a thumb against his chest in dismay. "How is it my fault?"

"You encouraged me. Don't you remember when we had our first talk? You said I ought to have more confidence in myself where women were concerned. You said, as I recollect, that I might turn from an ugly duckling into some kind of swan."

"And have you?"

"Let's put it this way. I'm well on my way to swanhood, thanks to you." Slade chuckled. "Ada thinks well of you. She told me so. She said you cut a fine figure. I hope you're not going to try to take her away from me."

"I'm not, son. That's a promise. Ada and me, we're just acquaintances. Ships that pass in the night, as they say."

"Well, then," Slade said, beginning to beam, "all I have to fret about is getting her out from under the thumb of her father. But I don't know how in the world I'm going to go about doing that."

Gabe had no advice to offer the obviously lovesick Slade. The boy would find a way out of his dilemma in time. He doesn't need any help from me, he thought. Young love always finds a way. He promptly changed the subject.

"I've been wanting to have a word with you, Slade."

"You have? About what?"

"The killing of Ed Brock for starters."

Slade stared at Gabe without saying anything.

"I was told that you were in the woods at the time Brock was shot to death."

"Who told you that?"

"Does it matter?"

"Yes, it matters. People on this wagon train, they sure do like to gossip. There's hardly a one of them that I've run into that doesn't get a thrill out of minding everybody else's business for them."

"Were you in the woods that day?"

"Who said I was?"

"Somebody who saw you there."

"I want to know who it was. Who was it accused me?"

"If you insist on knowing—it was Gwen Landon. She was also in the woods, and she told me she saw you there. Now will you tell me if she was right or wrong about that?"

"Gwen Landon's not somebody who ought to be casting first stones at anybody. She's got her own sins to cover up, she has. I told you about her and George Gordon. They're running around behind Mrs. Gordon's back. Everybody and his brother knows that. Everybody, that is, except Mrs. Gordon, or so I understand."

"I'm not so sure that the one thing has anything to do with the other. Were you in the woods when Brock was shot?"

Slade hesitated. He nodded. "I was."

"What were you doing there?"

"I was supposed to meet Ada there. She was late. Then Mr. Brock got himself shot and people came a'running and I never did get to keep my planned rendezvous with Ada."

"Did you see anybody else in the woods at the time?"

"No. I was in a kind of hiding place Ada and I had found. I couldn't see anybody from in there. I thought nobody could see me, but I know now I was wrong on that count."

"Did you hear the shot?"

Slade shook his head.

"Miss Landon also told me you had a reason to kill Brock, but she didn't tell me what that reason was."

"That's not true!"

"It's not? You mean Miss Landon lied to me?"

Slade started to say something but stopped. He gazed at Gabe, tension tightening his features. Finally, "I might as well tell you. If I don't, you'll probably just go back and ask her. She knows all about it. She overheard Mr. Brock talking to me one day. It seems he used to scout for the Army. That's how he found out I was drummed out of the service."

"What for?"

"I lost my temper one day and hit an officer, came close to killing him. Knocked his block off, I did. He didn't come to for nigh onto an hour. They court-martialed me and threw me out on my ear. Mr. Brock teased me about that trouble in my past that I've been trying to keep hid. He had his eye on Ada, too, in case you didn't know. He warned me to stay away from her. When I said it wasn't at all likely I'd do that, he told me he knew I'd been court-martialed and he knew why. He asked me what Ada would think of somebody who'd been thrown out of the Army in disgrace. Would she think I was worth bothering with then? I asked him not to tell her. I begged him not to. He just laughed at me."

"Did you kill him to keep him from letting the cat out of the bag about you and your military career?"

Slade's eyes widened. He shook his head. "No, I never did!"

"You had a good reason to kill him. To keep him from spoiling things between you and Ada."

Reluctantly, Slade said, "I suppose that's true enough. But Lord A'mighty, I wouldn't *kill* him on account of that."

As Gabe turned to leave, Slade said, "Don't you believe me?"

Did he? Gabe wasn't sure. He said, "I heard what you told me."

He spent the next several hours—until it was close to midnight—visiting one wagon after another and questioning their owners concerning their doings on the day of the two deaths. Many of the people he talked to had alibis which seemed to eliminate them as suspects. Others, not so fortunate, nevertheless inpressed Gabe as unlikely suspects for one reason or another. All of them had no motive for killing Brock that he could uncover, and most insisted that they had not left the protection of the circled wagons during the hours before dawn on the day in question.

Before calling it a night, Gabe decided to pay a visit to George Gordon. He wondered as he made his way through the darkness that was dispelled here and there by lanterns or banked fires if he would find Gordon at his wagon. Or would he be with Gwen Landon?

He was mildly surprised to find him sitting on one of his rockers outside his wagon. The man had his head back and his eyes closed as he gently rocked. He seemed to be dozing. But, as if some sixth sense had alerted him to Gabe's presence, his eyes snapped open and he squinted up at his visitor without offering a greeting.

"Evening," Gabe said to him. "I thought you might be in bed."

"What can I do for you, Mr. Conrad?"

"I've been talking to folk about the murders," Gabe began. "I thought I'd finish off the night by talking to you about them."

"What do you mean?"

"Well, I wanted to ask you a question or two, if you don't mind. Like, where were you when Brock was murdered?"

"Where was I when—" Gordon closed his eyes as he

considered the question. "I'm not really sure. I think I was—no, that was the day before. I was—" He opened his eyes and met Gabe's stare. "I was milking our cow as I recall when I heard the excitement which turned out to have been caused by Miss Landon's discovery of the wagon master's body. When I finished—when Bossy's bag was empty—I gave the milk to my wife and went into the woods along with just about everybody else."

"When was the last time you saw Brock alive?"

Gordon frowned thoughtfully. It took him a full minute before he answered. "It was while I was milking Bossy. He passed me by. He said something about being on his way to relieve himself. 'If I don't do it soon,' I remember him saying, 'my back teeth will start to swimming.' "

"Was anyone with him?"

"He was alone."

"Did anyone follow him into the woods?"

"I don't know. I was busy with Bossy. I had my hands full, so to speak."

Gabe matched Gordon's smile.

"Wait a minute," Gordon said suddenly. "I did see someone go into the woods a minute or two after Brock did."

"Who was it?"

"Hal Slade."

"Was he armed, could you tell?"

"He was too far away for me to tell whether or not he was carrying a gun."

"Was anyone with him?"

"No one that I could see."

"I was told you were on guard duty the night my friend, Purcell, was shot to death and his gold stolen. Is that true?"

"It's partially true."

"Partially true?"

"I was standing guard from midnight to dawn that

night—and morning, to be quite correct about it. A fellow by the name of Soames had the previous dusk to midnight shift."

"Did you happen to come anywhere near the camp Purcell and I shared while you were on duty?"

"I can't say for sure, Mr. Conrad, for the simple reason that I don't know where your camp was located."

Gabe told him the camp's location.

Gordon shook his head and began to build a quirly. "No, Mr. Conrad, I was riding west of there most of that night."

"Were you alone on watch?"

"Yes. Our former wagon master was in the habit of assigning just one man to each shift. Maybe he should have had someone standing guard during the day as well, considering how things turned out for him."

Gordon's wry comment went unremarked by Gabe who said instead, "Thanks for taking the time to talk to me."

"Anytime, Mr. Conrad," Gordon said as he lit his quirly and blew smoke into the air.

"How's your missus? Is she still feeling under the weather?"

"I'm sorry to say she is. But I'm hoping her sickness will soon be over."

"I'll bid you good night, Mr. Gordon. Tell Mrs. Gordon I give her my best regards."

"I'll do that."

Gabe had just awakened and was pulling on his boots the following morning when he heard a cry erupt some distance away. He turned his head to see what the disturbance was. At first, he saw nothing. But then a woman appeared at the rear of the Gordon wagon and went running across the open expanse of ground enclosed by the circled wagons. He caught just a glimpse of her face. It was enough to see the fear that was etched upon it.

He quickly got up and sprinted after the woman. When he caught up with her, he seized her arm, bringing her to a halt.

"Mrs. Perkins, what's the matter?" he asked.

"Oh, Mr. Conrad, we're doomed, every last soul amongst us is!"

Gabe heard the hysteria in her voice. He saw it flashing in her anguished eyes. "What are you talking about?"

"It's Martha Gordon. She's got it!"

"Got what?"

"Cholera!" Mrs. Perkins cried and burst into tears.

Gabe took her in his arms and held her as she sobbed, her face buried against his chest. A chill had gone through him at the sound of the dread word she had just spoken. Cholera, he knew from past bitter experience, killed. Not everyone who contracted the dread disease died, but all too many did.

He himself had once come down with cholera when he was twelve years old and living among the Oglala with his mother. He still recalled the nausea and the debilitating diarrhea the disease had inflicted upon him so that at times he almost wanted to die to end the terrible torment he was suffering. He had lain on a pallet in the lodge he shared with his mother and had grown increasingly weaker and weaker as the days passed.

The tribe's shaman had been summoned, and he had made his medicine, chanted his holy words over Gabe, but nothing he did or said had done any good. Not those holy words, not the tonics made from herbs that his mother administered to him, and not the prayers she had said over her stricken son as he lay tossing and turning in the throes of his illness.

"Doomed," Mrs. Perkins repeated, drawing back from Gabe and gazing at him as if he might know some secret that would allay her fears.

"Is Martha Gordon the only one who's sick?" he asked.

"I don't know. I went there this morning to see how she was feeling—she'd been sickly—and the minute I laid eyes on her I knew. My mother died of cholera, Mr. Conrad. Oh, I am so afraid. Not for myself but for my young'uns."

Mrs. Perkins turned and fled.

Gabe went in the opposite direction, the one Mrs. Perkins had come from, toward the Gordon wagon.

He heard weeping as he neared it. He hesitated a moment, not altogether willing to expose himself once again to he wiles of his old enemy whom he had once defeated, and then pulled back the canvas flap so he could see inside the wagon.

It was George Gordon who was weeping. He was kneeling beside his wife who was lying on a straw-stuffed mattress. His face was buried in his hands. His shoulders shook.

Gabe looked from him to Martha Gordon. The woman's eyes were closed. A blanket covered her trembling body.

"Hitch up your team," he ordered Gordon.

The man's hands dropped away from his face. He stared in shocked disbelief at Gabe. "Hitch up my team? Why? You're sending us away, is that it? Because my wife's got cholera? You're a heartless son of a bitch, Conrad, a heartless cold-blooded bastard, is what you are!"

"Shut up and listen to me, Gordon. I'm not sending you and your wife away. At least, not the way you mean. But I want you to drive your wagon out of the circle and away from all the others. Find yourself a secluded spot nearby and stay there. We've got to try to contain the disease if we can, and that's one way we can maybe manage that."

"I think she's dying," Gordon moaned, looking down at his wife.

"She's not dead yet so don't go getting out the shovel

to bury her before she is," Gabe said sharply, trying to shock Gordon into acting rationally.

Gordon rose and stiffly climbed out of the wagon and began to hitch his team to it.

Gabe left him to make the rounds of the other emigrants' wagons. When he had finished doing so sometime later, he was stony-faced and trying not to give in to his rapidly growing sense of impending disaster.

During his rounds, he had discovered four others who were also sick with cholera. There was no denying now what he was facing.

A cholera epidemic had descended upon the wagon train, and before it was over people would be dead. Some of the sick would never see California. Some of them were right now nearly at the end of their long journey. He stood with his shoulders slumping as he tried to absorb the enormity of the problem he and the others were facing.

A man named Abel Kearney came up to him. There was a stunned expression on his face.

"Mr. Conrad," he said hesitantly, "what are we going to do?"

Gabe drew a deep breath and told him.

CHAPTER NINE

"There's no denying that we're facing trouble, serious trouble," Gabe told the assembled emigrants he had sent Abel Kearney to bring together so he could address them. "But you folk have faced trouble before on the trail west. You can face the epidemic we've got amongst us, too."

Although he knew he sounded and appeared confident—his voice was strong and his gaze was steady—Gabe wasn't all that sure that he believed his own words. Could these people really face the deaths of their loved ones? He knew that people were going to die. He could hear the weeping of some of the women among the people facing him. He could see the naked fear on the faces of supposedly strong men.

"There are things we can do to fight the disease," he continued, his eyes shifting from one face to the next and then on to the next, trying to instill strength in his listeners.

"What things?" a man called out from the back of the crowd. "My wife's laid low and you're saying there are things we can do. *What* things?"

"I'm not lying to you," Gabe told the man. "How many of you men were in the Army during the war?"

There was silence in response to the totally unexpected question.

Gabe repeated it.

All of the young men raised their hands, and one or two older men also raised theirs.

"What's the Army got to do with what's sickening us?" the man who had spoken earlier cried impatiently.

"Cholera thrives on unsanitary conditions," Gabe stated. "So we've got to do two things to start off with. First, we've got to isolate the people who have the disease as much as we can. The second thing we have to do is dig a trench for everybody to use like the kind the Army uses in the field.

"You men who've done some soldiering know what I'm talking about. I want a detail to dig a trench far away from camp. We'll all use that trench until it comes time to fill it in and dig us another one. Do I have any volunteers?"

Several men raised their hands.

Gabe surveyed the crowd. "I don't know how much you folks know about the enemy we're about to fight—"

"We know it destroys," a woman in the crowd said. "We know it kills."

"We *don't* know where it comes from," another woman said.

"It kills when food or water or utensils and such get contaminated by the people who've come down with the disease," Gabe explained. "So the main thing we've got to fight with is sanitation."

"Sanitation?" an incredulous Abel Kearney inquired. "You mean to say the only thing we can do is keep ourselves and our things clean and we'll survive? I don't know that I believe that, Mr. Conrad, I've got to say straight-out."

"Believe me, Kearney," Gabe said, "I'm telling you the truth. I want you all to make sure you boil spoons

and plates and cups and clothes—things like that which
come into contact with an infected person. If someone
sick can't eat all the food you fix for him, then that food
has got to be taken out and thrown away in the trench
we're going to dig."

Gabe went on to explain other precautions that could
be taken to try to prevent the spread of the disease,
including the isolation, insofar as was possible, of all
those infected. By the time he had finished speaking
and the men who had volunteered to dig the trench
were about to depart to get their picks and shovels, he
thought he sensed a stirring of hope in the emigrants
facing him.

But that hope was abruptly shattered with the sudden
appearance of a haggard Henry Ferguson who moved
wraithlike among the people gathered around Gabe.

"He's dead," Ferguson stated, his voice flat.

"Who's dead?" Gabe asked him.

"My son, Tom. He just died. He stopped soiling himself and the bedclothes and he—he just went. Now my
other boy, Billy, he's sick. I don't want him to go the
way of his brother, Mr. Conrad, but what can I do? I
don't know what to *do!*"

Gabe put a hand on Ferguson's shoulder. "I'm sorry
to hear about Tom. We'll have to bury him right away.
I hope you understand."

"I don't understand!" Ferguson wailed, his eyes rolling in his head. "I don't understand *anything* anymore!"
He raised his eyes until he was gazing heavenward. He
raised both arms, his fingers quivering as they seemed
to reach for the sky. "Why, oh Lord, *why?* Why must
you afflict me in this fashion? I have lived a God-fearing
life. I have done harm to no man. Lord, will you take my
last living son from me?"

Gabe nodded to a man standing near Ferguson. The
man took Ferguson by the arm and began to lead him
away.

"Don't do it, Lord!" the wild-eyed Ferguson suddenly screeched. He shook his fists at the sky. "I'll damn you if you *dare* do it!"

"And so we commend our sister, Evelyn, to Thy tender loving care, oh Lord, amen."

Gabe joined in the chorus of amens uttered around the grave of the ninth victim of the cholera in the four days since Martha Gordon became the first person to come down with the disease.

He turned away from the grave as some men began to fill it and the mourners drifted away, some to the wagons outside camp where their relatives or friends languished and others to their wagons where health still prevailed among the occupants.

He sat down on a barrel that seemed to belong to no one and dropped his head into his hands as weariness almost overcame him. He had helped nurse the sick and bury the dead almost without pause for sleep during the past four days, and he felt worn-out. He had witnessed the onset of severe muscular cramps in the people stricken with cholera and had held their heads while they vomited violently in the terrible clutches of the illness. He had seen children die, including the second son of Henry Ferguson, Billy, which had reduced the child's parents, especially the child's father, to a helpless state of soul-shattering grief. Billy had died within an hour of Ferguson's first son, Tom. Other victims lasted longer but not always much longer. But some, for reasons no one understood, recovered, although one who had done so had subsequently died. The survivors were so weakened they could barely eat or sit up. To Gabe, California had begun to seem a world away. He wondered at times if he would ever get any of the emigrants to that fabled land. Perhaps they would all die. Perhaps he would.

He looked up when he heard a woman speak his name. "Beg pardon, Mrs. Lane? I didn't catch what you said."

"I said you look worn-out, Mr. Conrad," Audra Lane observed. "You should get some rest, or you'll be no good to yourself or anyone else either."

"I'll try to get some sleep soon."

"I brought you this." Mrs. Lane held out a chamois bag sewn shut and tied with a long strip of rawhide. "It contains dried asafetida out of my home medicine chest. Some say asafetida wards off cholera."

Gabe rose and took the offering. "I'm obliged to you, Mrs. Lane, I truly am. A person needs all the help he can get in the face of an epidemic like the one we got on our hands." He tied the chamois bag around his neck.

His action brought a satisfied smile to Mrs. Lane's face.

"People are doing whatever they can to·try to stay healthy," he remarked. He pointed to a man in the distance who was breaking open shotgun shells and consuming the gunpowder they contained. "I saw one woman yesterday dosing herself with something called Doctor Lloyd's Soothing Syrup for the Lower Tract."

"I say believing something will work is half the battle," Mrs. Lane said. "So I want you to believe that that bag of asafetida will do the trick for you. Don't forget. You've still got a job to do. Namely, get us to California."

Gabe couldn't help but sigh. "Do you think there'll be anybody left to go to California once this scourge passes?"

Mrs. Lane didn't answer his question. Instead, she patted the chamois bag hanging around his neck and said, "Get some rest, Mr. Conrad, before you fall asleep on your feet."

When she had gone, Gabe went to where he had left his gear and started to unpack his bedroll, intending to take Mrs. Lane's advice. He was shaking out his blanket when Jack Murdoch came striding up to him.

"Is she here with you?" he barked without preamble.

"Is who here?"

"My daughter is who I'm talking about. I can't find her no place."

"She's not here," Gabe said wearily as he spread his blanket on the ground.

"I'll find her," Murdoch vowed darkly, "and when I do, I'll whup her to pieces."

Gabe watched the man storm off. He was about to lie down on the ground when a thought occurred to him. He left his blanket where it was and began to make his way through the camp. Ten minutes later, he had not found who he had been looking for, and no one had been able to tell him the whereabouts of Hal Slade.

It was not until he stopped at the Kearney wagon where Abel and his wife, Miranda, remained healthy but fearful of the future and what it might hold that he learned that Miranda Kearney had seen Hal Slade riding out of camp early that morning.

"Was he alone?" Gabe asked her.

"Yes, he was."

"Which way did he go?"

"South," Miranda said.

Gabe hurried back to get his gray. He got the animal ready to ride in record time and then left the camp. He wasn't sure if there was a connection between the disappearance of Ada Murdoch and the departure from the camp of Hal Slade or not. But he intended to find both of them for the simple reason that either one of them could have been involved in the deaths of Ed Brock and Oscar Purcell. When he found them, he intended to bring them back with him.

He searched the ground for sign as he rode south but found none until he had passed over a stretch of rocky terrain and out onto a sandy plain which stretched as far as the horizon. There he found hoofprints leading south. He began to follow them. They met with other prints about a mile farther on. There the ground was torn up as the riders who had been traveling south and west respectively had stopped to talk. He rode on, following the new southward trail made by both horses.

It vanished where the riders who had made the trail had ridden into a streambed. But not entirely. Gabe rode along the stream's bank, his eyes on the water through which he could see the stream's sandy bottom. He spotted an overturned stone. Then another one. Ten minutes later, he heard the faint sound of a waterfall up ahead of him. He approached it and halted at the point where the stream spilled over a ledge. He got down from his gray and leaned over the ledge.

He smiled.

They were down below him, Hal Slade and Ada Murdoch. Both of them were naked as snakes, he observed, as they cavorted in a pool formed by the waterfall. Their horses lapped at the water.

He hunkered down and continued watching them, feeling envious of Slade for having captured the affections of Ada Murdoch.

As the laughter of the happy pair drifted up to him, Gabe resigned himself to losing Ada. He rose and, leading his horse, made his way down into the valley below him. As he emerged from a stand of cottonwoods, the laughter of the pair in the pool died. They stood there staring at him, water dripping from their bodies.

"What are you doing here?" a sulky Ada asked Gabe.

"I think you both know what I'm doing here," he replied.

"Did my pa send you to find me?" she asked petulantly.

Gabe shook his head.

"Then what for do you want to come up on us like a thief in the night like you just went and did?" a surly Slade asked.

"I've come to take you two back to camp."

Gabe's remark was met with groans. Ada and Slade exchanged downhearted glances.

"Can he do that?" Ada asked her companion.

Gabe didn't hear the young man's muttered answer. "Why don't you two get dressed?" he suggested.

They climbed out of the pool and began to dress, neither of them speaking. But both of them gave Gabe glowering looks from time to time.

He was ready for it when Slade finally made his move. As the boy grabbed for his gun which lay holstered beside the pool, Gabe's gun cleared leather seconds sooner than Slade could aim or sight.

"I don't want to have to shoot you," he told Slade.

The boy lowered the barrel of his .44.

Ada and Slade finished dressing then and boarded their horses which had wandered to a thin patch of shade not far from the pool.

"My pa's going to kill me," Ada declared mournfully and a little fearfully as she rode beside Slade, her dress hiked up on her thighs, her lithe legs exposed for Gabe and the rest of the world to see.

"How come you rode out here after us?" Slade asked Gabe. "What's it to you if we run off and get married?"

So that was it, Gabe thought. The young lovers had eloped. "Oscar Purcell and Ed Brock are both dead," he said, "and I still don't have a notion who killed them."

The meaning of his statement took a little while to sink in.

When it did, Ada's eyes opened wide and she exclaimed, "You don't mean to say you think we did those two men to death, do you?"

"Well, do you?" Slade asked when Gabe did not immediately answer Ada.

"You might have," he said. "One or both of you together."

"*I* certainly didn't!" Ada cried hotly, giving her young companion what Gabe decided might have been a suspicious glance.

"Neither did I," Slade blustered a moment later. "If you think either one of us killed Mr. Brock or that friend of yours, well, I can tell you you're dead wrong, Mr. Conrad."

Maybe so, Gabe thought. Maybe not. He changed the subject. "How come you two went and ran off like you did? You could have got married when you got to California."

"I figured it was high time I was moving on," Slade said.

"And he asked me to move with him," Ada announced with pride and glowing eyes she turned on Slade.

"I figured," Slade continued, "that what happened to me in the Army was sure to become public knowledge sooner or later and when it did I'd probably not be wanted on the wagon train. I'd be disgraced and turned out. I figured you or Gwen Landon would spill the beans about me for sure."

"I never would have," Gabe said. "Tell me something. Why did you hit your superior officer and knock him for a loop, Slade? You didn't tell me that part of the story and I'm curious."

Slade gave Gabe a speculative glance before saying, "There was this fellow, a private like me, name of Lester Slykes. Lester and me, we were friends. Good friends. Now Lester, he wasn't the smartest fellow in the whole wide world, but he had him a good heart and he was the kind of fellow would give you the shirt off his back should you happen to be in need of it.

"One day Lester forgot to carry out an order our superior officer, Lieutenant Carter, gave him. When the lieutenant found out that Lester hadn't done what he'd been ordered to do, he pitched a fit. He had Lester bucked and gagged. To teach him a lesson, he said."

Gabe knew all about the punishment called bucking and gagging which was frequently administered in the Army. A prisoner would be placed in a sitting position with his hands bound together and slipped over his knees. A rifle would be inserted beneath the prisoner's knees and over his arms. A bayonet would be tied in his mouth to gag him.

"Bucking and gagging's a cruel thing to do to a man," he commented.

Slade gave him a sidelong glance. "It's an *awful* thing to do to a man, truly awful. Lieutenant Carter left Lester out on the parade ground bucked and gagged in the hot sun. After a few hours of that torment, Lester was sobbing like a baby somebody had beaten, but Lieutenant Carter turned a deaf ear to him.

"So I took it upon myself to free my friend. Lieutenant Carter caught me in the act. He ordered me to buck and gag Lester all over again. I refused. And then I guess I lost my head. I hit Lieutenant Carter with my fist and knocked him into the middle of next week. He was out cold. They threw me in the guardhouse and, well, you know the rest."

"The other day Hal told me what happened to him in the Army," Ada volunteered. "He decided he didn't want me hearing it from anybody else."

When she spoke next, there was a note of defiance in her tone. "I think what he did for his friend was fine and wonderful, that's what I think. It was a brave thing to do, not something to be ashamed of."

"I agree with you, Ada," Gabe said.

Slade beamed at both of them.

They rode on in silence for some time and then Gabe said, "We're not far from camp. Before we get there, I have something I want to say to you two."

Ada and Slade waited expectantly and somewhat nervously to hear what he was going to say.

"If you decide to light a shuck again, I'll go after you the same as I did this time. Next time when I catch up with you, I might not be inclined to act kindly toward you. Is that clear?" Gabe glanced at Slade who nodded and then at Ada who, reluctantly, also nodded.

They rode on.

"Now what do you suppose that horse is doing up there?" Gabe asked softly a few minutes later as if he were talking to himself.

"What horse?" Slade asked, his brow furrowing as he stared in the direction Gabe was gazing. "I don't see any horse."

"Me neither," Ada said.

"Look sharp," Gabe advised them. "Up there—to the left and in among those loblolly pines. See it? The black with the blaze?"

"Now I can see it," Ada said. "It was playing hide-and-seek in the trees."

Gabe headed for the black, motioning his companions to follow him. When the trio reached the pines and rode in among them, they looked around but saw no rider. Gabe did see some tracks where boot heels had dug deep into the ground. He began to follow them. They led him deeper into the pines where the shadows were thicker.

At first he thought he was looking at just another shadow caused by some shifting of the branches overhead. But then he knew it was no shadow he was seeing.

"Oh, my heavenly Lord!" Ada exclaimed as she and Slade rode up on either side of Gabe and she saw the grim sight he was staring at.

"Lordy, that's Mr. Ferguson," Slade breathed as if afraid to speak out loud in his normal voice in the presence of death.

Henry Ferguson hung at the end of a knotted rope from one of the pines. His body revolved slowly as the wind played with it. Then it revolved in the opposite direction under the wayward direction of the wind.

"He hanged himself," Ada whispered, awed by the sight before her. "Now why would he do a terrible thing like that?"

Gabe thought he knew the answer to her question. "Him and his family have been facing hard times of late. Harder, it looks like, than he could bear."

"Henry, where are you?"

"Somebody's coming," Ada said.

"A woman," Slade said.

She came running through the sun-dappled woods, her hair askew and her eyes anxious. Mrs. Ferguson skidded to a stop when she saw her husband's hanging body. Her right hand slowly rose to cover her gaping mouth. She closed her eyes and then opened them again as if hoping that the horror she had seen had been nothing more terrifying than a hallucination.

She screamed. Then she screamed again.

Gabe slid out of the saddle and hurried over to where she was standing. "Don't look," he advised her. He took her by the arm and started to lead her away. "Bring my horse," he told Slade.

Mrs. Ferguson broke free of Gabe and ran to her husband. She threw her arms around his legs and pressed her face against them. She sobbed uncontrollably.

Gabe beckoned to Ada.

She slid off her horse and went to Mrs. Ferguson. She put her arms around the distraught woman and whispered something in her ear. At last, Mrs. Ferguson let herself be drawn away from her husband's body. Ada led her over to Slade's horse. She gave Slade a meaningful glance.

He got out of the saddle and helped Mrs. Ferguson into it. He drew the reins over his horse's head and was about to lead it in the direction of the camp when Mrs. Ferguson said in a sepulchral voice, "Poor Henry, he just couldn't bear up under what the Lord saw fit to inflict upon us. When Billy died, that was the last straw. I knew something terrible was going to happen to him. He didn't act right. He had notions about things. That the Lord was hounding him. That there were demons tormenting him. He told me once he had to escape from it all. When he went missing, I came looking for him, fearing the worst."

Gabe nodded to Slade as Mrs. Ferguson covered her face with her hands and began to weep again.

Slade led his horse in the direction of the camp with Ada riding behind.

Gabe went to the tree from which Ferguson's body hung suspended. He cut Ferguson down and threw the man's corpse over the withers of the black before stepping into the saddle of his own horse and riding out, leading Ferguson's horse and its grim burden.

The next day, while the healthy members of the emigrant community attended the burial of Henry Ferguson, Gabe moved silently and stealthily through the encampment. He went from empty wagon to empty wagon, some of them emptied by death, some by the ceremony taking place in the distance, as he diligently searched through the wagons for Oscar Purcell's gold.

He found no gold. Only two wagons remained to be searched. They were those belonging to the Widow Lane and George Gordon. He anticipated no difficulty with Mrs. Lane; he was sure she would grant him permission to search her wagon. But the Gordon wagon was another matter altogether.

Martha Gordon remained bedridden in it so he could not search it now. He doubted that George Gordon would grant him permission to search the wagon anyway. His belief was founded on another belief—that Gordon might well have killed Purcell and stolen the man's gold the night Gordon was standing guard duty for the emigrant train.

But, at the moment, Gabe was painfully aware that he had only his suspicions to go on. Nothing concrete. But if he found Purcell's gold in the Gordon wagon . . .

In the distance, the burial ceremony was ending. Gabe picked out Mrs. Lane as she moved slowly away from the grave site and headed toward her wagon. He moved quickly to join her.

"I see it worked, Mr. Conrad," she told him when he joined her.

He was puzzled for a moment. Then he said, "Oh, you mean this?" He touched the chamois bag that hung around his neck, the one she had given him which contained dried asafetida. "Well, maybe it did at that," he said with a smile. "Since I'm still reasonably hale and hearty."

"You still look tired though," Mrs. Lane observed. "You're not getting enough rest, are you?"

"I reckon not. But that's on account of there's lot of things to be done. Tending the sick. Burying the dead. Lots of things."

"Like bringing back eloped lovers."

"Oh, you heard about that, did you?"

"I heard. You ought to be ashamed of yourself, Mr. Conrad. Interfering in the course of young love."

"Well, you know what folk say, ma'am. The course of true love never runs smooth. I guess I helped to prove the truth of that saying in the case of young Slade and Ada."

"I hope their love affair works out. Hal Slade is a nice boy. He's given me a hand more than once when I was in sore need of one. Just as George Gordon's done. You tend to expect such behavior of a mature man like Mr. Gordon, but not of a youngster like Hal who is straddling the fence between boyhood and being a man. But I think he'll be good for Ada Murdoch. He'll settle her down. From all I've heard and seen, she could stand some settling."

Gabe said nothing.

"Young blood runs hot, Mr. Conrad," Mrs. Lane continued casually. "It drives some youngsters wild at times. But that doesn't mean those young folk are bad ones. It just means that nature can play dirty tricks on folk. Especially young folk."

"Mrs. Lane, I wonder if you'd mind if I searched your wagon?"

"Search my wagon? Why, Mr. Conrad? Did you lose something?"

"You're pulling my leg, ma'am."

"You want to know if that gold you've been hunting in our wagons will turn up in mine, don't you?"

"I do. I don't really think it will, but I've got to satisfy myself that I've made a thorough search for it. I hope you understand the position I'm in."

"You're welcome to search my wagon anytime. How about right now?"

"Right now would be fine and dandy."

They made their way to the Lane wagon. Mrs. Lane remained outside it while Gabe entered and thoroughly searched it. He found no gold. But he did find a framed photograph of a young man wearing a three-piece sack suit and standing beside a lovely young woman on whose shoulder his hand rested. The woman wore a veil over her hair. In her hands was a small bouquet of violets.

"Did you find what you were looking for?" Mrs. Lane asked as Gabe emerged from her wagon a few minutes later.

"I didn't nor did I expect to, as I said. But I did come across a picture which I think must be of you and your mister."

"That picture was taken on our wedding day, Mr. Conrad. Wasn't Arthur Lane a handsome young fellow though?"

"Yes, I reckon you could say that about him. The reason I mention the picture is because I wanted to tell you that you looked as pretty as can be in it."

"How gallant of you to say so, Mr. Conrad."

Gabe unfastened the lid of the barrel that was roped to the outside of the Lane wagon and thrust his hand into the small quantity of grain it contained.

He found no gold hidden in the feed barrel.

"I'm running out of feed for my stock," Mrs. Lane told him with a worried look on her face. "I'm going to have to break a cardinal rule of mine against borrowing. I always say if you don't have and can't afford, don't borrow. Do without."

"But you're not talking here about satisfying your own needs," Gabe pointed out. "You're talking about borrowing grain to keep your stock alive."

"Very good, Mr. Conrad." Mrs. Lane waited a moment before saying, "Mr. Conrad, you're not listening to me, are you?"

"What? Oh, beg pardon, ma'am. I was just watching the Gordons. It looks like Mrs. Gordon is feeling better. Her hubby's just carried her out of their wagon and put her in her rocker."

"Oh, that's a good sight to see, isn't it? I was so afraid we were going to lose Martha. Praise the Lord, she's gotten better. But then so have one or two other folk who came down with the cholera. I'm beginning to believe— dare I say it—that the scourge has run its ugly course."

Gabe had begun to think and hope the same thing during the past twenty-four hours. "If you'll excuse me, Mrs. Lane, I'll go pay a call on the Gordons."

When Gabe reached the Gordon wagon, George Gordon had disappeared. He greeted Martha Gordon and inquired politely after her health.

"I'm feeling ever so much better, thank you, Mr. Conrad," the woman replied in a voice that was a faint echo of her normally robust one. "I think I may be out of the woods where the cholera is concerned. At least, I hope I am."

"I hope you are too, Mrs. Gordon." Gabe hesitated a moment before asking, "Would you mind if I searched your wagon? I've been searching all the wagons while you were sick, looking for the gold that was stolen from my friend."

Martha Gordon's brow beetled. "Do you think the gold is in our wagon? Do you think George stole it?"

"I don't know where it is or who stole it," Gabe replied. "Like I said, though, I'm trying hard to find it."

"Well, I don't know," Martha Gordon said nervously, her fingers fidgeting in her lap. "I mean I don't think George would want me to give you permission to do a thing like that without him knowing about it first."

"Where is he? I'll go ask his permission to search the wagon."

"I don't know where he is at the moment. Why don't you come back at another time when George is here, Mr. Conrad? Would you do that please?"

Gabe nodded and left. But that night, as fires burned in the camp and people strolled about or visited together, he returned to the Gordon wagon. He rapped on the tailgate as the yellow light of a lantern filtered faintly through the wagon's canvas cover.

"Who is it?" George Gordon called from inside the wagon.

"Gabe Conrad."

The cover was pulled aside, and Gordon's head and torso appeared in the light-filled opening. "We were just getting ready for bed. Is something the matter, Mr. Conrad?"

Gabe explained that he had come to search the wagon if he could obtain permission to do so and apologized for disturbing the Gordons at such a late hour. "But yours is the last wagon on my list," he concluded, "and I'd like to have a look through it now if you don't mind."

To his surprise, Gordon beckoned him inside, even holding the canvas aside to ease his entry. Inside he found Martha Gordon wearing a pale cambric nightdress, her hair let down and her feet bare.

"I'm sorry to bother you at this hour," he told her.

"Do you feel strong enough to step outside, Martha?" her husband inquired. "Mr. Conrad wants to search our wagon." As he was helping his wife leave the wagon, Gordon said to Gabe, "My wife told me you were here earlier today on the same mission. We saw you searching the Widow Lane's wagon, and she said that you also wanted to search ours. So go right ahead, Mr. Conrad. Let us know when you're finished."

"I won't be long," Gabe promised as the Gordons left the wagon. He began his search at once, going through boxes filled with clothes and knickknacks, gunnysacks full of foodstuffs, and tarpaulin-covered furniture. He was about to leave some time late when he saw, out of the corner of his eye, something flash in the light of the lantern. He turned his head—and saw nothing. Had he imagined seeing the flash? Slowly, he shifted position and looked around the area. Still nothing.

Then, as he reached out and raised the lantern's wick so that more light filled the wagon, he saw it again, the flash that had previously caught his eye.

He hunkered down and thrust his hand under the edge of a tarpaulin that hid a ceramic chamber pot painted with pink cupids. There was nothing in the chamber pot. But there was a faint trace of gold dust lying on the floor in front of the chamber pot just under the edge of the tarpaulin.

It glittered as Gabe stared at it as if it were taunting him. He searched a second time through the wagon, more slowly and very carefully this time.

He found no more traces of gold. He looked down again at the faint traces of gold dust lying so innocently on the floor. They were almost unnoticeable. If I'd come here in the daytime, he thought, it'd be dim in here. Chances are I'd have never seen that dust.   ·

Where, he asked himself, had the gold dust come from? There was no sign of Purcell's poke anywhere in the wagon. Maybe the dust was the faint residue of some treasure that belonged legitimately to the Gordons. But, if that were the case, where was that treasure now? He was certain it was not in the wagon.

"Mr. Conrad," Gordon called from outside the wagon. "My wife's very tired and there's a chill in the air out here. If you're quite finished—"

"I am." Gabe called back and climbed out of the wagon. "I thank you both for your indulgence."

Before either of the Gordons could say anything, he walked away, his thoughts racing, his mind in turmoil.

CHAPTER TEN

Gabe spent a restless night, his occasional brief periods of sleep troubled by images of a faceless thief and that thief's stolen gold. When he awoke, as he did often during the long night, it was to lie under the stars and go over and over in his mind all the things he had learned since joining the wagon train about what might have happened to Purcell's gold at the hands of whoever had stolen it.

He recalled his talk with Gwen Landon. And his initial talk with Martha Gordon. The latter had insisted that her husband had joined her as soon as he finished his stint as guard and scout for the sleeping emigrants. But Gabe had seen Gordon leaving the Landon wagon when he had first arrived at the encampment. When he had talked with Gwen, she said Gordon had visited her to borrow some coffee beans.

But then he had learned from Hal Slade that there were rumors abroad among the emigrants that Gwen Landon and George Gordon were having an adulterous love affair.

Clearly, one of the women was lying about that morning. But which one? And why?

Then there was the murder of Ed Brock that still
baffled him. Why had the former wagon master been
slain? Brock had been going to tell Gabe something
he thought Gabe should know, something Brock had
suggested might shed light on the murder of Purcell. But,
before he could do so, he had been killed himself. Did
someone want to prevent him from telling Gabe what he
knew? Or had there been another reason of which Gabe
was unaware that had motivated Brock's killer?

An image of the brawny Jack Murdoch drifted men-
acingly in Gabe's mind. Murdoch was a man who might
very well have murdered Brock because he believed the
wagon master had violated his daughter, Ada. Had Brock
actually done so or had Ada gone with Brock of her own
free will? Gabe realized he might never know. Which
didn't matter, he decided. What did matter was that
Murdoch, a man possessed of a violent temper who
had even threatened to kill Gabe at one point, might
well have sought and found vengeance with the aid of
a gun.

There was also the possibility that Ada herself might
have done in the wagon master. Gabe had once known
a woman who avenged herself on a man who had raped
her by slitting his throat from ear to ear one dark night.
Was Ada capable of killing? Given the circumstances,
Gabe speculated, she might very well be. Especially if
she had inherited her father's volatile temper.

Then there was Hal Slade to consider. Had he killed
Brock to keep the man from revealing the truth about
his dismissal from the Army? Gabe wasn't sure that that
was a sufficiently strong motive for murder. It wouldn't
have been for me, he thought. He would have let Brock
tell his tale if he felt he had to and then taken the conse-
quences, whatever they might have turned out to be. But
Slade was young and, as Mrs. Lane had remarked, the
young harbored hot blood. Add to all that, Slade's abrupt
departure from the train. Had it really been merely an

elopement? Or had it been an elopement and something else as well? Had Slade decided to light a shuck with Ada to avoid punishment if it were ever discovered that he had killed Ed Brock?

Gabe's head whirled. There could be others—many others—who had a reason to kill the wagon master. Reasons he knew nothing about and was not likely to ever uncover.

There was, for one example, Audra Lane. As unlikely a suspect on the surface as could be, the Widow Lane might have harbored hidden hatred for Brock. Perhaps she blamed the wagon master somehow for the death of her husband during the journey west. Gabe scoffed at his own speculation, tending to dismiss the Widow Lane as a suspect, although he knew he shouldn't.

The murder of Oscar Purcell was another matter entirely. There, at least, the motive for the murder was clear: Purcell's cache of gold. But finding the killer and thief was not proving to be easy.

Which brought Gabe to considering the one seemingly solid piece of evidence he had discovered that quite possibly pointed a finger at George Gordon as the murderer of Purcell. He was thinking of the traces of gold dust he had found in the Gordons' wagon.

He was suddenly brought up short in his thinking. Suppose the gold dust he had found in the Gordons' wagon had indeed once belonged to Purcell. Did that mean that George Gordon had killed Purcell and stolen the man's gold? Not necessarily. It didn't prove guilt beyond the shadow of a doubt. The presence of gold dust on the floor of the Gordon wagon might indicate that Martha Gordon had killed Purcell for the treasure. Or, as Gabe had been thinking when he first discovered it, it might mean only that the Gordons had some gold that belonged to them and the dust was not connected in any way with Purcell's gold—or his murder.

Gabe turned over on his side and tried to go back to sleep. But, as his thoughts continued to whirl, they effectively kept sleep at bay. He was still awake when the first hint of dawn lit the eastern horizon, throwing the mountain peaks looming in the distance into ghostly relief against the pearl-gray sky.

He spent most of the morning checking the conditions of the emigrants who had survived their bouts with cholera. All were weak yet not only willing but eager to resume their journey west.

He learned two other things of importance during his visits to the people in his charge. Almost all were short of food both for themselves and for their livestock as a result of the unexpected delay caused by the cholera which had seriously depleted the little food and grain they had left for the remainder of their trip.

Speaking of the starving stock, Abel Kearney lamented, "Look ye yonder, Mr. Conrad." He pointed to the lush grass growing all around the camp. "I don't understand it. My oxen won't graze that fine grass. You'd think it was poisoned or some such thing. Not a blade of it will the beasts touch."

"I can explain that, Kearney," Gabe declared. "What you're looking at, it's buffalo grass. The buffalo feed on it. It grows short—about an inch to an inch and a half high at most. Now that just happens to be a fine height for buffalo, but it's not a bit good for oxen."

"Why is it not, pray tell?"

"Buffalo's mouths are made different than oxen's. That is to say, their lips are. Buffalo have a long lower lip and a short lower jaw so they can graze low-growing grass with ease. Oxen, on the other hand, are even-lipped, and they just can't get at it the way the buffalo can."

When Gabe had completed his tour of the train, he asked for someone to volunteer to turn over an ox or a cow to be slaughtered for food to be shared by the needy. At first, there were no volunteers, but then Mrs. Lane stepped forward.

"You can take my milch cow, Mr. Conrad," she offered. "The old girl's not done well on this trip, and my guess is that she'll expire before she finally gets down out of these mountains. I have to say that her imminent demise is my fault in large part. I've had my livestock on painfully short rations these past few days. They'd have all died off on me by now if it hadn't been for the kindness and generosity of Mr. George Gordon who yesterday graciously gave me some of his own grain to feed my critters with after he heard me say I was running short."

Spontaneous applause erupted in acknowledgment of Gordon's selfless act of sharing.

"You're sure you want to do this, Mrs. Lane?" Gabe asked.

"It's hard to satisfy two oxen and a cow with the little grain I've got on hand even though Mr. Gordon gave me as much of his as he could spare. If I only have to feed the two oxen instead of them and my cow as well, I just might make it on the grain I've got stored in my feed barrel at the moment."

Gabe gave an order, and two men detached themselves from the assembled emigrants and disappeared. When they returned, they were leading Mrs. Lane's cow.

She patted its head as it passed her.

"Get a good grip on her," Gabe told the men as he drew his knife.

When the two men had both gotten firm holds on the cow's head, Gabe walked around in front of the animal.

Mrs. Lane turned away so she would not have to witness what was about to take place. So did several other women.

Gabe deftly drew his knife from left to right across the dewlapped neck of the cow.

The animal tried to bellow, but all that emerged from its mouth was a strangled cry. It tried to break free of the two men holding it but succeeded only in causing a geyser of blood to spurt from the gaping wound Gabe had made in its neck.

The cow's knees began to buckle. It dropped down upon them. It tried to rise but failed to do so. It tried to raise its head but could not do that either. As its eyes glazed and its head dropped down, the men holding the animal let it slump to the ground where it lay with its life's blood flowing from it.

Gabe wiped the blood from his knife on the grass as the cow's heart stopped pumping the blood out of its body.

"I have a few more things to say before the butchering begins," he announced. "We'll pull out after we make our nooning. Before we do, I want every wagon's load lightened. Get rid of everything—especially heavy things like pianofortes and anvils—that can be replaced once you get to California."

There were mutters of protest.

"It's got to be done," Gabe insisted, "and you all know it does. Your oxen and mules are weak as it is. They'll die on you, and then you'll be lucky to get just yourselves to where you're going. A cutting away of unnecessary possessions now can save you a lot of grief later, I promise you.

"I suggest the able-bodied folk amongst you do what you can to make your outfits trail-worthy. Now's a good time to oil your wagon covers to help keep out the rain. Check your wheels and fix any that need it. Grease your axles with tar or tallow. When you get your share of meat, pack it in barrels of bran if you've got some so it won't be so quick to spoil. Dry some of it. I'll inspect each wagon before we pull out to make sure it's fit for the trail, is that understood?"

When no one protested, Gabe nodded to the men who were standing by with their knives at the ready. They began the butchering.

Later, as Gabe made his own nooning, he stared into the fire he had built and over which he had boiled a vegetable stew in an iron kettle he had borrowed from the Widow Lane.

Something bothered him as he ate. Something he couldn't quite put his finger on. Something that was as troubling as a toothache. He tried to ignore it but found he could not.

He chewed thoughtfully, going back over the events of the day to try to identify what it was that was nagging at him. His efforts were, in the end, unavailing. He silently swore and continued eating, burning his tongue as a result of not paying attention to what he was doing. He swore a second time—out loud this time.

He looked around quickly, but there were no women near him to hear his profane words. His glance fell on Mrs. Lane who was standing on a milking stool as she spread linseed oil on her canvas wagon cover.

Mrs. Lane.

Now what was it that made him think that whatever it was that was bothering him had something to do with her? He had borrowed a kettle from her. Earlier he was among the people who had heard her volunteer to sacrifice her cow for the good of the hungry on the train. . . .

What was bothering him, he suddenly realized, had something to do with what she had said at that time. He tried to remember exactly what it was she had told the assembled emigrants. She had talked, he recalled, about the difficulty of feeding three animals on a limited amount of grain. She had said that even with the additional grain that George Gordon had so generously given her to tide her over for the remainder of the journey, she still feared that she might run short so she was willing to hand over her cow to be slaughtered.

That was it! That was definitely what had been gnawing at the edges of his mind, Gabe realized. He stood up so fast that he almost spilled the bowl full of stew in his hand. He quickly placed it on the ground and then, his meal forgotten, he made his way over to the Widow Lane's wagon.

When he reached it, he proceeded to make small talk with the woman. He thanked her for lending him her kettle. He promised to return it "as clean as a whistle." She told him she was eager to be on her way again. And so on.

Gabe made a show of sniffing the air.

"What's wrong?" she asked him. "Is something wrong, Mr. Conrad?"

"Maybe there is." He unfastened the lid of her feed barrel and looked down into it. He sniffed again. Then he thrust his hand all the way down to the bottom of the barrel. He brought up a handful of grain and held it up to his nose.

"This feed's turned bad," he announced, restoring the barrel's lid.

"Oh, no!" Mrs. Lane exclaimed from her perch on the milking stool.

"I'm real sorry," he said, "but it'll have to be thrown out, feed and barrel both. You wouldn't want to go and put good feed in this barrel now that it's been contaminated by feed gone bad."

Before Mrs. Lane could say anything more, Gabe untied the barrel from the side of the wagon and carried it over to the edge of a deep draw. He hurled the barrel down into the draw where it came to rest against the trunk of one of the pines growing there.

An hour later, he visited each of the emigrants' wagons to see that each was fit for the trail. He made it a point during his visits to tell everyone on the wagon train that they should check their supply of feed for their livestock because Mrs. Lane's had gone bad on her. They all promised to do so.

By one o'clock the wagon train was once again on the trail to California's Sacramento Valley. At four o'clock,

Gabe, riding in front of the first wagon in line, held up a hand to call a halt.

When the wagons stopped, he rode the length of the train telling everyone that they would make camp early so that those people who were still convalescing from the cholera could get a good rest without any further exposure to the rigors of travel for the remainder of the day.

Then, as drivers began to circle the wagons, Gabe rode into the woods bordering the camp. Once within the shelter of the trees, he galloped back the way the train had just come.

By the time he reached the spot where the previous camp had been, his gray was sweaty and its barrel was heaving with its heavy breathing. He dismounted and led his horse behind a pile of boulders where it could not be seen by anyone approaching from the west. Then he made his way to the draw where he had thrown Mrs. Lane's feed barrel. He climbed down into it and took cover among a stand of pines.

He didn't have long to wait. Less than half an hour later, as the sun dropped out of sight behind the mountains, he heard the nickering of a horse high above him. He waited, his eyes on the rimrock above the draw.

A figure appeared and began a hasty descent into the draw, arms flung outward for balance, eyes on the feed barrel lying at the base of a pine tree. Within seconds, the descent was complete and the person Gabe had been waiting for sprinted across the draw and dropped down on both knees next to the barrel. Gabe watched as the lid of the barrel was removed and a gunnysack extracted from the feed in which it had been buried. The kneeling figure began to chuckle.

As George Gordon's chuckle became raucous laughter, Gabe stepped out of the cover of the trees, his gun in his hand and leveled at the kneeling man.

Gordon must have sensed Gabe's presence behind him. His head turned. When he saw Gabe and the gun in Gabe's hand, he leapt to his feet and went for his own revolver.

"Drop it!" Gabe ordered before Gordon's gun had completely cleared leather.

Gordon defiantly disobeyed the order. He slid out his gun and fired at Gabe, missing him.

Gabe fired, hitting Gordon in the right hand, causing him to drop his weapon. As Gordon clutched his wounded hand, Gabe walked around him. He picked up the man's gun and thrust it into his waistband. Then he picked up the gunnysack and slung it over his shoulder.

He gestured with his gun and Gordon began to climb out of the draw with Gabe right behind him. When they reached the level ground above, Gabe gestured again and Gordon boarded his horse.

"Head for those pines over there," Gabe ordered him. "If you try to make a run for it, I'll drill you, so be warned."

A silent Gordon did as he had been told.

When they reached the trees, Gabe got his gray and stepped into the saddle. "I'm taking you back to camp, Gordon. Move out ahead of me."

Only then did Gordon speak. "Look, Conrad, maybe we can work something out."

"Like what?"

Hope flickered in Gordon's eyes. His nostrils flared. "I'll split it with you. Sixty-forty."

"I take it you mean *I* get the forty percent."

"Right. A full forty percent."

Gabe shook his head.

"Alright!" an exasperated Gordon cried. "We'll split it right down the middle. Fifty-fifty."

When Gabe said nothing, Gordon asked, "Well, what about it? Fifty-fifty's fair."

Gabe shook his head again.

"What the hell do you want, Conrad? *All* of it?"

"I want none of it," Gabe answered. "Let's go, Gordon. I'm not known as a patient man. If you keep shooting your loud mouth off, I just might run out of patience and shoot you."

Gordon, his shoulders slumping and his wistful eyes on the gunnysack slung over Gabe's shoulder, turned his horse and rode west into the setting sun.

Gabe followed him, his gun still in his hand and leveled at his captive's back.

Some curious and startled stares greeted the pair as they rode into the camp some time later. There were questions in the eyes of the emigrants and it finally fell to Hal Slade to ask them.

"What's going on, Mr. Conrad? What for have you got your gun trained on Mr. Gordon?"

Gabe gestured, summoning the people, and then ordered Gordon out of the saddle. He got down to the ground himself. When an expectant crowd had gathered, he answered Slade's questions.

"This is the murderer and thief I've been looking for. He killed my friend and stole my friend's gold. Here it is." Gabe held up the gunnysack.

There were gasps from some of the members of his audience.

"I caught him red-handed," Gabe added. "You all know that I searched your wagons looking for this gold. The next to last wagon I searched yesterday belonged to the Widow Lane. That's where I found the gold."

"Were they in cahoots, Mr. Gordon and the Widow Lane?" Jack Murdoch asked.

"I stole no gold!" Mrs. Lane protested loudly and angrily, her eyes flashing. "How dare you accuse me of such a thing, Mr. Conrad!"

"Hold on," Gabe said. "I'm not making myself clear. Let me explain. I searched Mrs. Lane's wagon like I said. But I didn't find the gold there—not then, I didn't. I happened to notice George and Martha Gordon watching me search the wagon. Him and his missus were outside their wagon at that time. Well, that didn't mean a thing to me at the time. Then I went over to the Gordon wagon and asked Mrs. Gordon—her husband was gone by then—if I could search her wagon. She said she'd have to ask her husband. When I went back late last night, both husband and wife agreed I could search their wagon. I found traces of gold dust inside it but no cache of gold."

"Then how come you say Mr. Gordon stole it and killed your friend?" a puzzled Hal Slade inquired.

"It wasn't till today that I put two and two together," Gabe said. "I strongly suspected all along that Gordon might be the guilty party but the presence of gold dust in his wagon didn't prove it. Then it hit me. He'd moved the gold after I searched the Lane wagon. He moved it to the Widow Lane's feed barrel."

Gabe glanced at Gordon. "Tell me if I've got it figured out right. When you filled her feed barrel, you also put this gunnysack full of Purcell's gold down at the bottom of it and made sure it was covered up with grain. I found it there. You knew I wouldn't be searching that wagon again, but you also knew I hadn't yet searched yours. So the gold was safe in the widow's feed barrel while I searched your wagon. You intended to retrieve it later the first chance you got."

When Gordon said nothing, Mrs. Lane questioned him. "Is what Mr. Conrad just said the truth?"

"It's the truth," Gordon admitted reluctantly.

More gasps came from the people in the crowd. Stony stares of disapproval were turned on Gordon.

"When I guessed what happened," Gabe said, "I set a trap for the thief."

"But you already knew who it was," Ada Murdoch piped.

"No, Ada, I didn't. Not for sure, I didn't. I had no proof that it was Gordon who had the gold and who had hidden it in the feed barrel, but I was pretty sure he was the one who had done it."

"So what sort of trap did you set for him, Mr. Conrad?" Slade asked.

"I went to the Widow Lane and—my apologies, ma'am—lied to her," Gabe answered. "I told her that her feed was spoiled, though it really wasn't. I threw the barrel—with the gold in it—down into that draw back by where we camped last night. Then I made the rounds of all the wagons and talked to you all. I made sure everybody—including the Gordons—knew that I'd chucked the widow's feed barrel into the draw."

"I don't see—" Ada ventured.

Gabe interrupted her. "Whoever hid the gold in the feed barrel, I figured, would come hunting it first chance they got. That's exactly what Gordon did. I was there—down in the draw—waiting for him when he did."

"You shot him," Gwen Landon noted, pointing at Gordon's wounded right hand.

"I did," Gabe readily admitted. "I had to. It was self-defense. He threw down on me."

Some of the members of the crowd edged closer to where Gordon was standing with his eyes lowered. They seemed fascinated by the man now that they knew what he had done.

Gabe, watching them, thought of the deadly attraction danger has for some people.

"You finished with your tale?" Jack Murdoch asked Gabe. "If you are, it looks like you ain't caught up with the killer of Ed Brock."

"You're wrong about that, Murdoch," Gabe said. "There stands the killer of Ed Brock." He pointed at Gordon.

Mrs. Gordon suddenly appeared from the depths of the crowd. She stood with her arms hanging limply at her sides as she stared at her husband. "Did you kill Mr. Brock, George?" she asked in a faint voice.

Gordon didn't answer her.

"You were there," Gabe said to him, "when I told Brock about the murder of Oscar Purcell the morning I joined the train. You heard Brock say he had something to tell me about that killing that he thought I'd find of interest. Only he was too busy at the time to talk to me about it. My guess is that he saw you sneak back to the train carrying this gunnysack full of gold that morning after you killed Purcell and stole his gold. Brock could have pointed the finger at you as a strong suspect in those crimes because you had no reason to be carrying a gunnysack at that time. You didn't want him doing that so you killed him. Have I got that right, Gordon?"

Gordon's eyes rose. He stared defiantly at Gabe and then at the people facing him. "You have, Conrad, damn you to hell! It happened like you said. Brock went into the woods to relieve himself. I followed him. That tale I told you about milking our cow at that time was a cock-and-bull story. I walked right up to Brock, put the cloth I'd brought with me up against his chest, and plugged him through it so nobody would hear the shot. Then I hightailed it back to my wagon."

"There's one thing that puzzles me," Gabe said. "I saw Jack Murdoch and Gwen Landon come out of the woods and later found out that Hal Slade had been in the woods at the time you killed Brock. Which made them suspects in my mind. But I never did see you come out of the woods. How'd you get out of there without anybody spotting you?"

A faint smile, almost a sneer, spread across Gordon's features. "That was easy. I cut north and came out of the woods where nobody'd see me. Then I sneaked back into camp and when the alarm was raised I went back into the woods along with everybody else like I'd never been there in the first place."

Gabe, recalling the camp and the way it had been set up at the time of Brock's murder—and his own position as he made his nooning that day—realized he wouldn't have been able to see Gordon leave the woods from where he had been sitting.

"It's not true, is it, George?" Martha Gordon asked plaintively. "Mr. Conrad's lying, isn't he? Everything he said is a pack of lies, isn't it?"

Gabe swore he heard Gordon snarl.

"No, my dear," the man snapped, "it isn't a pack of lies. Everything Conrad said is true. If it hadn't been for him, I would have gotten away with it." Gordon's baleful gaze returned to Gabe.

"But, George," his wife persisted, "why? Why did you do it? We're a far piece from being rich, but we had enough money to make a new start in California. We had each other, George. I don't understand any of this."

"That's because you're stupid, my dear," Gordon muttered.

Martha Gordon recoiled as if her husband had struck her.

"I intended to make a new start in California. That's true enough. But that new start did not include you. I intended to make a new start with the woman I love."

"The woman you love?" Martha Gordon swayed until a woman standing next to her put out a hand to help steady her.

"Gwen Landon is the woman I love," Gordon announced and turned to stare fondly at her.

"He's a liar!" Gwen screeched. "Don't believe a word he says."

Gordon looked suddenly crestfallen following her outburst. "But, Gwen, you and I—It was for you that I stole the gold. For us. When I came upon that man, Purcell, gloating over his gold that morning when I was out on the scout, I knew instantly what I was going to do. And I knew exactly why I was going to do it. You were glad

I had done it. You told me so when I got back to camp that morning and joined you in your wagon.

"You even helped me plan the murder of Ed Brock when I thought he was going to expose me," Gordon continued, his voice rising. "When I told you I thought Brock knew something that could harm me in the matter of the murder, you were the one who suggested I kill him."

"No!" Gwen cried, her face ashen.

"Yes," Gabe said. "I think I get it now. There was that matter of Brock's coat being buttoned up the wrong way over the cloth you used to silence your shot, Gordon."

Before he could say anything more, Gordon, still staring intently at Gwen, said, "We went into the woods when we saw Brock go into them. We figured that was our chance to get rid of him. I shot him and then Gwen buttoned his coat—"

"The way a woman would button a coat," Gabe interjected.

"And then after I made a run for it, she pretended to find the body. We figured everybody would think Brock had died of another heart attack like the one he'd already had on the trail so they wouldn't ever see the bullet hole in him. And they wouldn't have if you hadn't noticed that Gwen buttoned his coat the wrong way," Gordon concluded, glaring at Gabe.

Gwen turned and started to run.

"Grab her somebody!" Gabe yelled.

Jack Murdoch seized Gwen by the arm so that she could not escape.

"Oh, George!" Martha Gordon suddenly wailed, her voice breaking. "Oh, *no!*" She fainted.

Abel Kearney, who was standing with his wife, Miranda, near Martha Gordon, caught her before she could hit the ground.

"Take her back to her wagon," Gabe instructed Kearney, who picked her up and carried her away.

"Gwen said she was proud of me for what I'd done," Gordon said to no one in particular. "She loved me, she said, every bit as much as I loved her. We were going to have a brand new life together in California. I planned to desert Martha and go away with Gwen once we got there."

Gordon, using his uninjured left hand, pulled a gun from the holster the man closest to him was wearing. He spun to face Gabe and barked, "Don't you move!" Then, swiveling his gun, sweeping the crowd, he snarled, "Don't *any* of you move!"

CHAPTER ELEVEN

"Hand over that sack," Gordon demanded, his eyes boring into Gabe's. "And drop those guns!"

When Gabe dropped his six-gun and the one he had taken from the killer, Gordon yelled, "Hand over that sack of gold or you're a dead man, Conrad!"

Gabe took a step forward and then another one. He stretched out his arm toward Gordon, the sack containing the gold in his hand. Then, as Gordon reached for it with his wounded right hand, Gabe thrust it at him, hitting him in the chest with the heavy sack.

In that instant, when Gordon was taken by surprise, Gabe followed up by using the sack to knock the gun from Gordon's hand and simultaneously kneeing him in the groin.

Gordon let out an anguished howl and doubled over, clutching his crotch. As he did so, Gabe formed two fists and brought them both down like a club on the back of Gordon's bent head. Gordon went down on his knees, still doubled over, gagging.

Gabe stepped back and tightened his grip on the gunnysack.

Gordon chose that moment to make one last move.

He seized the gun he had dropped and fired wildly at Gabe who ducked, letting the bullet pass harmlessly over his head.

Before Gabe could straighten up, Gordon tore the gunnysack from his hand and fired a single shot. Then he ran.

Gabe was surprised when no bullet slammed into his body. He quickly turned, picked up his gun, took swift but sure aim, and fired.

Gordon's hands shot up into the air. The gunnysack fell to the ground as his body arched backward. His fingers clawed the air. He fell to the ground and lay there, his body jerking spasmodically.

Gabe walked over to him. By the time he reached Gordon, the man was no longer moving. His open eyes stared sightlessly at the sky.

"Is he—" Ada Murdoch asked from somewhere behind Gabe.

"He's dead," Gabe said tonelessly after feeling for a pulse in Gordon's neck and finding none.

"So is she," Ada said.

Gabe retrieved the gunnysack and asked, "Who's dead?"

Ada pointed at the lifeless body of Gwen Landon which lay facedown in the dirt some distance away.

Slade, standing beside Ada, put an arm around her and said, "That last shot Gordon got off. That's what killed her."

"I thought he was shooting at me," Gabe said.

"Not that time, he wasn't," Slade said. "He took aim straight at Miss Landon."

Gabe's gaze shifted from Gwen Landon to George Gordon. He thought of the trail of dead bodies that had led to this moment when he was safely in possession of the gold he had been seeking for so long.

Oscar Purcell. Ed Brock. Gwen Landon. And, finally, George Gordon.

• • •

Just before eleven o'clock the next morning, the wagon train crested a hill, and the emigrants saw the fertile Sacramento Valley lying below them. A spontaneous cheer rose from their throats and seemed to reverberate in the sunny air.

Gabe rode over to where Hal Slade was standing with Ada as her father glowered sullenly at both of them from a few feet away.

"Slade," he said, "you're in charge as of now."

"Me?"

"I'm leaving," Gabe explained. "You and the rest can make it on your own at this point. You think you can take charge of the wagon train?"

"You bet I can, Mr. Conrad. But I have to say I'm sorry to see you go."

"I've got business to see to."

Ada winked at Gabe as she said, "I bet it has to do with a woman, don't it?"

Gabe pointed a playful finger at her and said, "Ada, honey, you got it right the very first time." Then to the assembled emigrants who were marveling at the valley below them, he said, "Hal Slade's taking over for me from here on in. I hope you folk will cooperate with him the same as you did with me." He glanced at Slade and said, "The train's all yours, son."

Slade's face was suffused with pride. He seemed to Gabe to have grown an inch or two in just the last few minutes.

As Slade rode away to begin leading the procession down the hill into the valley, Ada spoke to Gabe. "I got something I want to say to you."

He waited.

"I'd like to get together with you one more time before you leave, but I can't. I hope you'll try to understand. I'm in love with Hal. I'm not going to be able to be— friendly—with any other fella now. When Hal and me get to the end of the trail, we're going to round us up a preacher and get ourselves hitched."

"I understand," Gabe said, assuming a mournful expression for Ada's benefit. "I mean, I realize you can't be—friendly—with me anymore, but I was wondering . . ." He let his words trail away.

"Wondering what?"

"If maybe a kiss might not be out of order? For old time's sake, let's say."

Ada smiled shyly and puckered her lips.

Gabe kissed them chastely. "Good-bye, Ada. I hope you and Hal will have a long and happy life together."

Was it a tear he saw in her eye just before he left her?

"Mr. Conrad," Martha Gordon said sharply as she emerged from the crowd. "I want to tell you I'm glad you're leaving. I can't stand the sight of you. Maybe my husband wasn't much, but he was all I had and you took him from me."

Gabe knew there was no defense he could offer that would satisfy her so he remained silent as she continued speaking, anger giving an ugly edge to her tone.

"You probably have guessed that I lied to you about George being with me the morning you joined the train. I suspected all along he was with Gwen Landon. I'd suspected for a long time about the two of them. But I didn't say anything to George. I was hoping he would get tired of her and come back to me. Now he never will. I hope you rot in hell for killing my husband, Mr. Conrad."

Gabe watched her turn and flee from him. He started to ride out when Jack Murdoch hailed him.

When Murdoch caught up to him on foot, he said, "I never really meant to kill you, Conrad."

"I'm glad of that."

"Raising a daughter like Ada without any help is a mighty tough task. A man—a father—has to stay on his

toes. I know Ada's—flighty—where men are concerned.
But I want you to know for a fact that Ed Brock really
did rape her. I came upon them while he was having at
her and she was doing her best to fight him off. It's a
true wonder I didn't kill him right there on the spot. Now
Ada's fixing to settle down with the Slade fellow."

"He's a good man, Murdoch. Give the two of them a
fair chance to make a life for themselves."

"Oh, I mean to do that. Though I don't relish the idea
of me becoming a grandpa which I reckon I'm sure to
turn into before long, knowing how young folk behave
while in the state of blessed marital bliss."

Gabe matched Murdoch's grin and then said, "Do me
a favor, will you? When I arrived I brought along a horse
and a mule that belonged to the friend of mine that was
murdered by Gordon. That's the pair of them over there
with the extra livestock."

"You're sure you want to get shut of them?"

"I am. Maybe you'll give them to your daughter and
son-in-law once they're ready to set up housekeeping.
Tell them they're a wedding present from me."

Murdoch nodded and offered his hand.

Gabe shook it and then moved out.

He halted again when he heard a woman call his name.
He looked back over his shoulder to find Audra Lane,
her homespun skirt swirling about her legs, hurrying
toward him.

"I wanted to bid you good-bye in a proper fashion,
Mr. Conrad," she declared when she arrived at his side.
"And to thank you for all you've done for us on behalf
of myself and the others."

"You're all more than welcome, Mrs. Lane."

"Abel Kearney volunteered to go back and get my
feed barrel for me which was right neighborly of him.
But never mind about me. What will you do now, Mr.
Conrad? Where will you go?"

"First off, I'm going to Sacramento. There's a lady

there that this gold belongs to." Gabe indicated the gunnysack resting between him and his saddle horn. "She's—she was—Oscar Purcell's fiancée. Before he died, he asked me to find the gold that Gordon stole from him and hand it over to his woman if I was successful in the search for it. I'm on my way to do that."

"Well, you won't need that anymore, I'll wager." Mrs. Lane pointed to the chamois bag she had given him which still hung around his neck.

Gabe's hand rose and touched it. "I don't think I'll throw it away for a while, ma'am. I think I'll keep it to remember you by."

Mrs. Lane smiled. "Safe journey, Mr. Conrad."

He left her behind, heading down the slope toward Sacramento.

When Gabe arrived in Sacramento, he headed straight for the livery barn. There, he was reasonably confident, he would be able to determine the whereabouts of Purcell's fiancée, Molly Hastings. Livery barn loafers always seemed to know everyone in town and everything that was going on or had gone on in town. It was a social center and, as such, despite its exclusively male makeup, was also a center of swirling gossip whether the town in which it was located numbered fifty or five hundred people.

When he reached his destination, he dismounted and strode up to the men gathered outside the livery in the shade of a chestnut tree. Some were whittling, others smoking, nearly all were talking.

"Beg pardon, gents," he said. "Maybe one of you can help me out. I'm looking for a lady named Molly Hastings. I thought you might know where I could find her."

Glances were exchanged. Several of the men gave Gabe appraising glances. He thought he heard someone snicker.

"Try the Nugget Saloon," one of the men suggested.

Gabe, somewhat taken aback by the suggestion, nodded. "The Nugget Saloon—which way is it?"

The same man gave him directions which he followed. He slid out of the saddle in front of the saloon, wrapped his reins around the hitch rail, and went inside carrying the gunnysack filled with gold. He found what he had expected to find in the saloon—smoke in the air, sawdust on the floor, and a half-drunk mob of mostly men.

"Molly Hastings," he said to a man seated by the door with a glass of beer on the table in front of him. "Is she here?"

The man pointed to a woman who was wearing a purple satin dress which barely reached her knees. It also barely covered her lush breasts. It was slit up one side, baring most of her right thigh. In her hair she wore an ornament of ostrich feathers and rhinestones.

Gabe hesitated. He recalled what Oscar had told him about his fiancée. Could this woman whom he recognized for the whore she so obviously was be the one Purcell had been planning to marry?

He went up to the bar and introduced himself to her. "Are you Molly Hastings?"

"Before I answer such a leading question," she simpered, "I have to know if you're the sheriff or a Pinkerton man. I wouldn't want to compromise myself."

"I'm a friend of Oscar Purcell's. He sent me to look you up."

"Oscar Purcell?" Molly's eyes narrowed. "Why did he send you to me?"

"He asked me to give you this." Gabe handed over the gunnysack.

Molly took the sack and opened it. Her eyes grew wide as she stared at its contents. She looked back at Gabe.

"I don't get it. What is this, some kind of joke?"

"It's no joke. Oscar found that gold and then he was killed. Before he died, he asked me to see to it that you got it."

"Well, I do declare!" Molly exclaimed. "Imagine that!"

"Oscar told me he was in love with you."

"Oh, he was smitten with me, there's no denying that. He kept badgering me to marry him. He was like a bad penny, Oscar was. He kept turning up with that hangdog look of his and begging me to be nice to him. Which I was when he had the money to pay me for being nice to him."

Gabe's face remained impassive but within him raged a dark impulse to reach out and strangle Molly Hastings.

"You're not kidding me are you, mister? Oscar really did send you here to give me all this lovely gold?"

"I already told you that."

"I was just checking to make sure I heard you right the first time. Well, well, well. So Oscar has made me a rich—if not an honest—woman."

"I'll be on my way."

As Gabe turned to leave, Molly said, "You told me Oscar got killed. Do you mind telling me how?"

"Another man shot him to death."

"Did you hear that, boys?" Molly called out to the men in the saloon. "You all remember Oscar Purcell, don't you? He was that silly man who couldn't leave off trying to court and carry me off even though I told him a hundred times if I told him once that I had no more use or liking for him than I'd have for a broken clock. Well, boys, it seems Oscar struck it rich and then he got killed. It also seems, according to Oscar's messenger boy here, that he's gone and made me the sole beneficiary of his estate and a very rich woman."

As Molly held up the gunnysack full of gold like a trophy she had just won, Gabe headed for the batwings.

He had almost reached them when he heard Molly say to the men who had gathered around to congratulate her, "So what do you know? Oscar Purcell, that longtime loser, has gone and lost the big one—namely, his life. Well, belly up to the bar, boys. Now that I'm filthy rich, thanks to poor dead Oscar, the drinks are on me."

Gabe grimly shouldered his way through the batwings and out into the night. He freed his gray, stepped into the saddle, and galloped away from the Nugget Saloon, slowing down only when he could no longer hear the sound of Molly Hastings's mocking laughter.

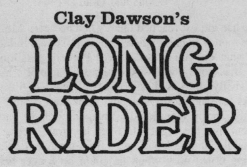